P9-CCD-847

TRANSFORMERS
REVENGE OF THE FALLEN

THE MOVIE UNIVERSE

LONDON, NEW YORK,
MELBOURNE, MUNICH, AND DELHI

SENIOR DESIGNER/BRAND MANAGER Robert Perry
MANAGING EDITOR Catherine Saunders
EDITORS Jo Casey, Julia March
PUBLISHING MANAGER Simon Beecroft
CATEGORY PUBLISHER Alex Allan
PRODUCTION EDITOR Siu Yin Chan
PRODUCTION CONTROLLER Nick Seston

First published in the United States in 2009
by DK Publishing
375 Hudson Street
New York, New York 10014

09 10 11 12 13 10 9 8 7 6 5 4 3 2 1
TD448—04/09

A catalog record for this book is
available from the Library of Congress.

ISBN: 978-0-7566-5172-5

Color reproduction by Alta Image, UK
Printed and bound by Lake Book, US

THE MOVIE UNIVERSE

BY SIMON FURMAN

CONTENTS

6 CIVIL WAR

8 TRANS-SCANNING

10 OPTIMUS PRIME Robot Mode

12 OPTIMUS PRIME Vehicle Mode

14 OPTIMUS PRIME Weapon Mode

18 MEGATRON Robot Mode

20 MEGATRON Vehicle Mode

22 MEGATRON Weapon Mode

24 SAM WITWICKY

26 HUMAN ALLIES

28 BUMBLEBEE Robot Mode

30 BUMBLEBEE Vehicle Mode

32 BUMBLEBEE Weapon Mode

34 BARRICADE Robot Mode

36 BARRICADE Weapon Mode

40 FRENZY Robot Mode

42 BLACKOUT Robot Mode

44 BLACKOUT Vehicle Mode

46 BLACKOUT Weapon Mode

48 SCORPONOK Robot Mode

50 JAZZ Robot Mode

52 JAZZ Vehicle Mode

54 **JAZZ** Weapon Mode
56 **RATCHET** Robot Mode
58 **RATCHET** Vehicle Mode
60 **RATCHET** Weapon Mode
62 **IRONHIDE** Robot Mode
64 **IRONHIDE** Vehicle Mode
66 **IRONHIDE** Weapon Mode
68 **STARSCREAM** Robot Mode
70 **STARSCREAM** Weapon Mode
74 **SIDESWIPE** Robot Mode
76 **SIDESWIPE** Vehicle Mode
78 **SIDESWIPE** Weapon Mode
80 **DEVASTATOR** Robot Mode
82 **DEVASTATOR** Weapon Mode
84 **SKIDS/MUDFLAP** Robot/Vehicle Mode
86 **THE FALLEN** Robot Mode
88 **THE FALLEN** Weapon Mode
90 **RAVAGE** Robot Mode
92 **JETFIRE** Robot Mode
96 **ACKNOWLEDGMENTS**

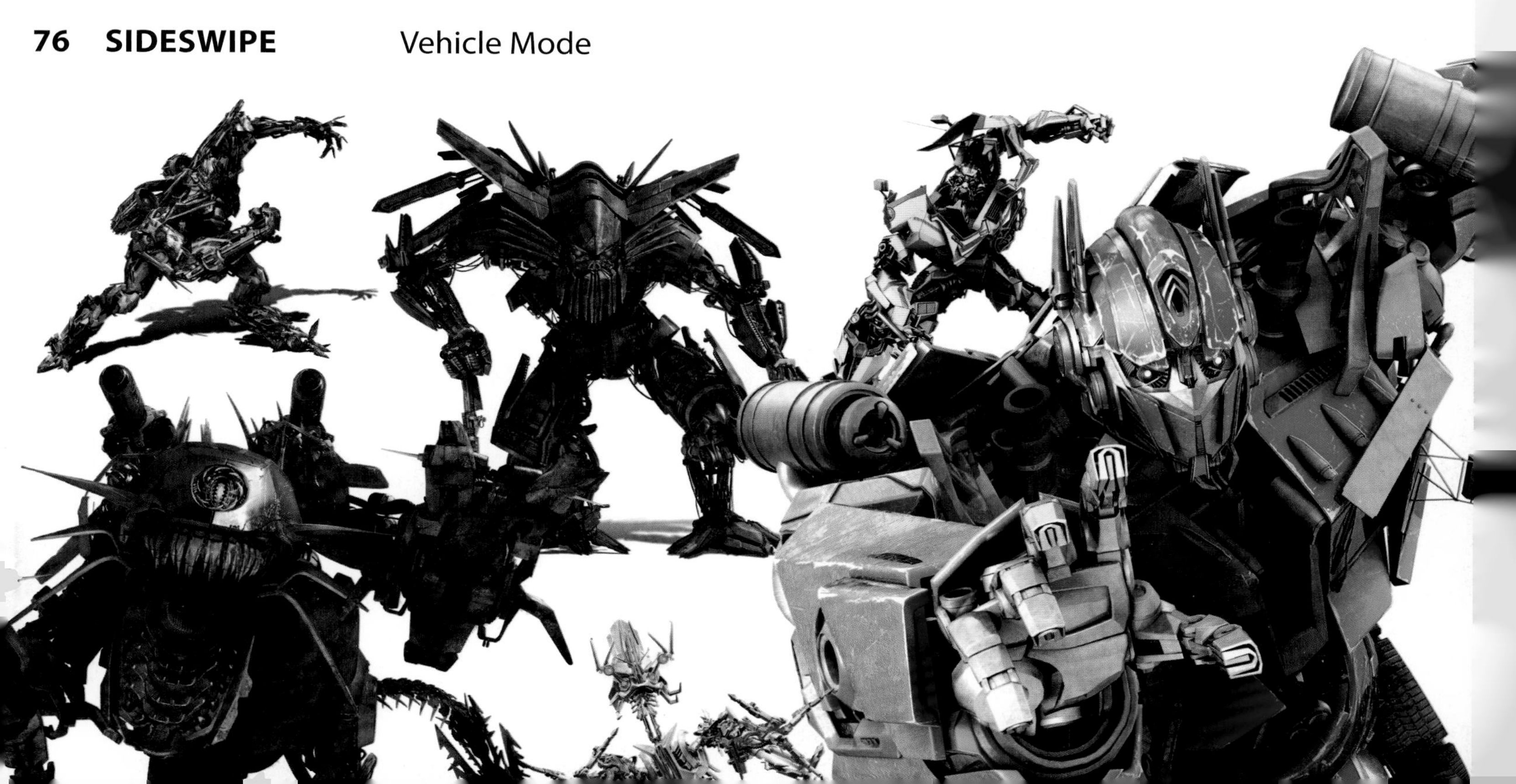

CIVIL WAR

IT ALL BEGAN ON CYBERTRON, a metal world of labyrinthine intricacy with its origins lost in the mists of time. Populated by monumental robotic beings—Transformers—able to adopt secondary vehicle and other modes at will, Cybertron was maintained and nurtured by the mysterious life-giving energy source known as the Allspark.

Autobot insignia

Decepticon insignia

DID YOU KNOW?
Although disguise and stealth are vital to Transformers, both factions—Autobot and Decepticon—always bear their insignia boldly even when in their vehicular (or other) modes.

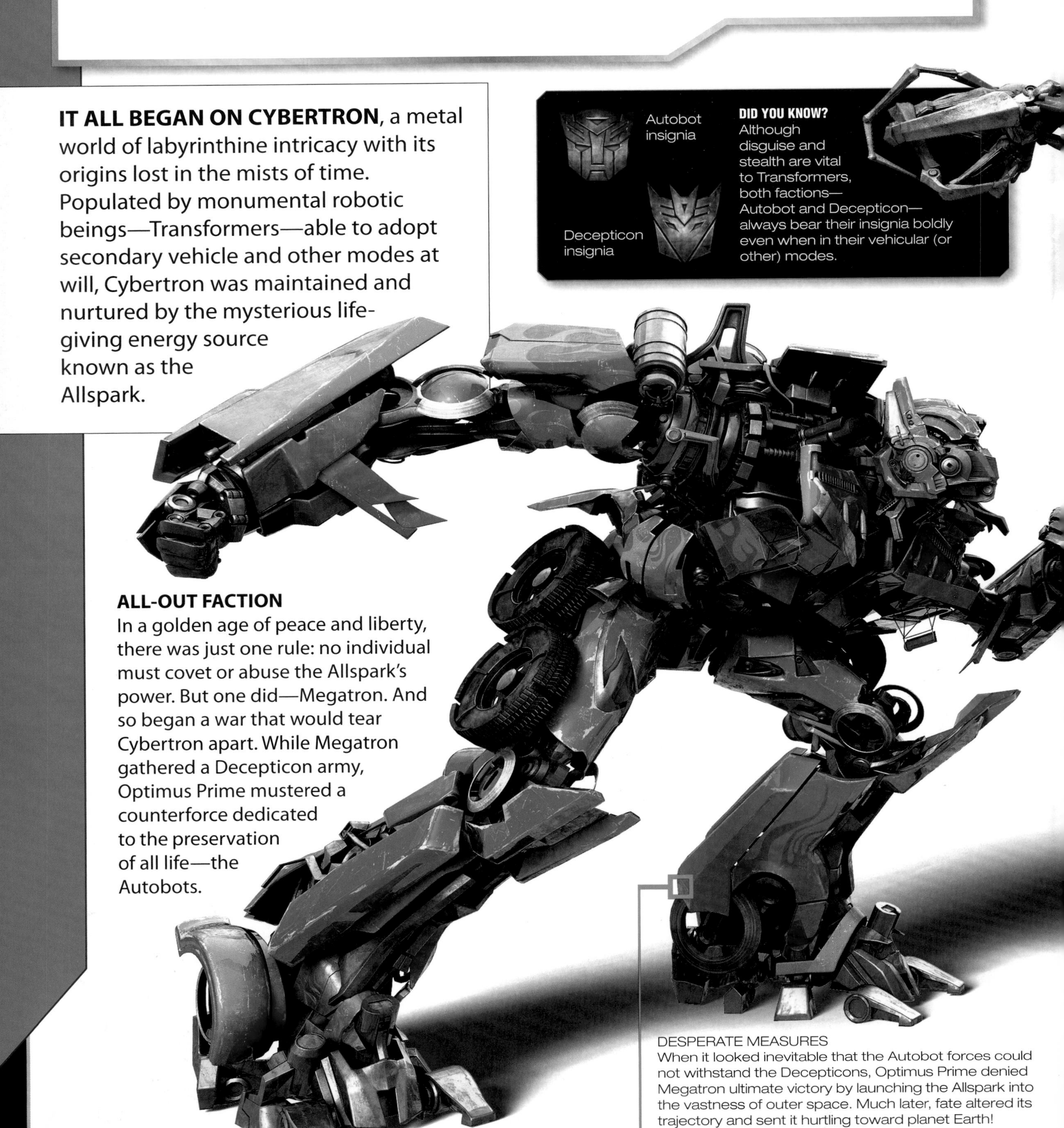

ALL-OUT FACTION
In a golden age of peace and liberty, there was just one rule: no individual must covet or abuse the Allspark's power. But one did—Megatron. And so began a war that would tear Cybertron apart. While Megatron gathered a Decepticon army, Optimus Prime mustered a counterforce dedicated to the preservation of all life—the Autobots.

DESPERATE MEASURES
When it looked inevitable that the Autobot forces could not withstand the Decepticons, Optimus Prime denied Megatron ultimate victory by launching the Allspark into the vastness of outer space. Much later, fate altered its trajectory and sent it hurtling toward planet Earth!

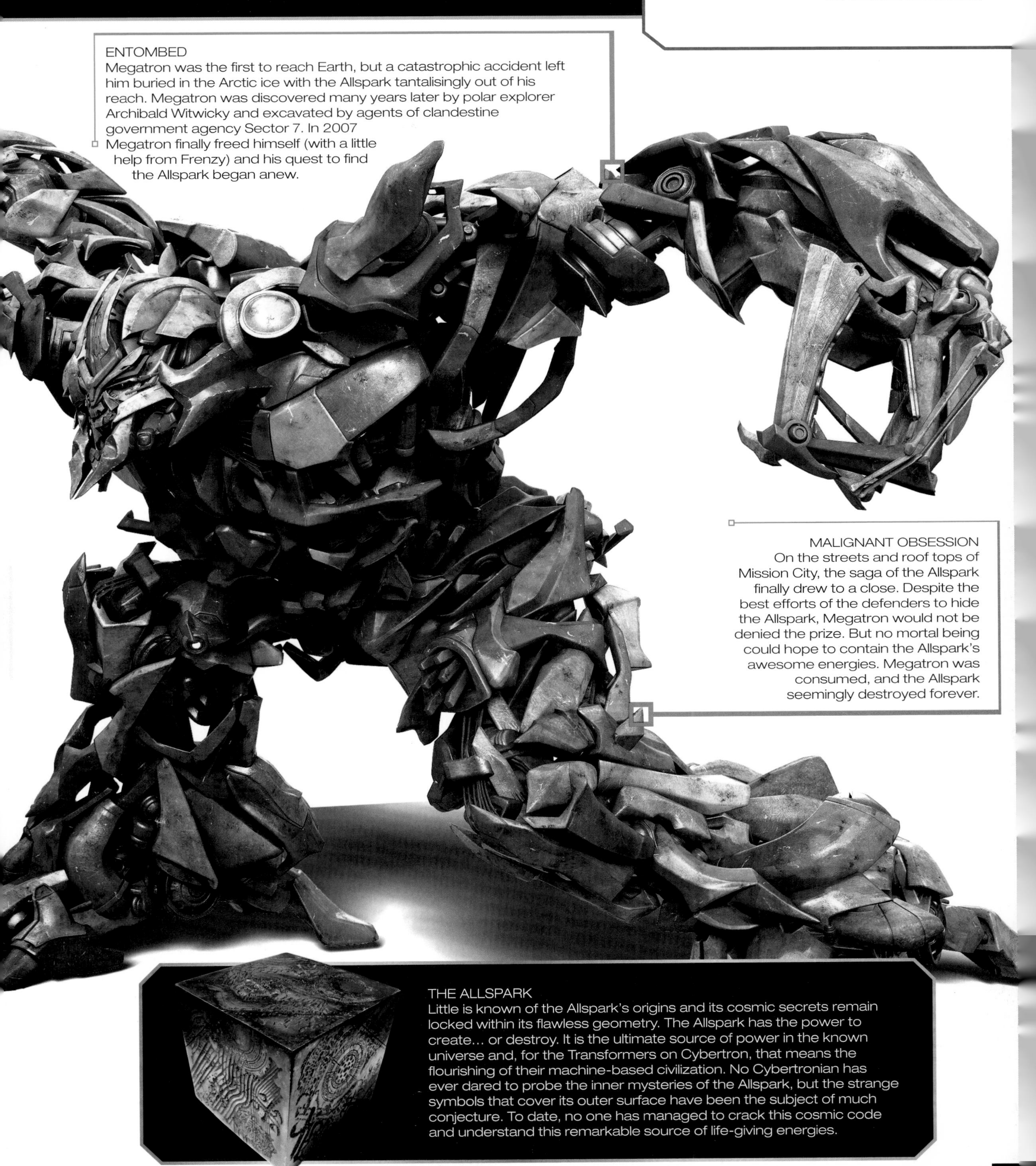

ENTOMBED
Megatron was the first to reach Earth, but a catastrophic accident left him buried in the Arctic ice with the Allspark tantalisingly out of his reach. Megatron was discovered many years later by polar explorer Archibald Witwicky and excavated by agents of clandestine government agency Sector 7. In 2007 Megatron finally freed himself (with a little help from Frenzy) and his quest to find the Allspark began anew.

MALIGNANT OBSESSION
On the streets and roof tops of Mission City, the saga of the Allspark finally drew to a close. Despite the best efforts of the defenders to hide the Allspark, Megatron would not be denied the prize. But no mortal being could hope to contain the Allspark's awesome energies. Megatron was consumed, and the Allspark seemingly destroyed forever.

THE ALLSPARK
Little is known of the Allspark's origins and its cosmic secrets remain locked within its flawless geometry. The Allspark has the power to create… or destroy. It is the ultimate source of power in the known universe and, for the Transformers on Cybertron, that means the flourishing of their machine-based civilization. No Cybertronian has ever dared to probe the inner mysteries of the Allspark, but the strange symbols that cover its outer surface have been the subject of much conjecture. To date, no one has managed to crack this cosmic code and understand this remarkable source of life-giving energies.

TRANS-SCANNING

CHIMERICAL BY NATURE, Transformers are constantly adapting their forms, either to blend in on other worlds or to physically traverse the vast distances between those worlds. In preparation for deep space travel, a Transformer will shed its current exo-structure and return to its most basic, stripped down configuration (protoform), before transforming into a protective, comet-like transition mode. Upon arrival, the Transformer trans-scans a vehicle or life form and reformats its protoform accordingly.

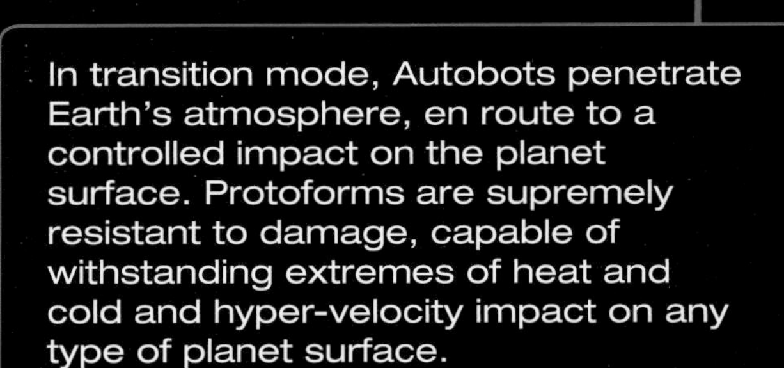

In transition mode, Autobots penetrate Earth's atmosphere, en route to a controlled impact on the planet surface. Protoforms are supremely resistant to damage, capable of withstanding extremes of heat and cold and hyper-velocity impact on any type of planet surface.

PROTOFORMS

[…]eart of every Transformer is […]oform. Rarely seen, the […]le infrastructure supports […]c reformatting process. […] on its own mass plus local […]erials, the protoform shifts […]ands, submerging itself […] new exo-structure. Upon […]t its destination, the […]m's built-in (automatic) […]begin to seek out a suitable […]f comparable size and mass.

[…]NAL MODE

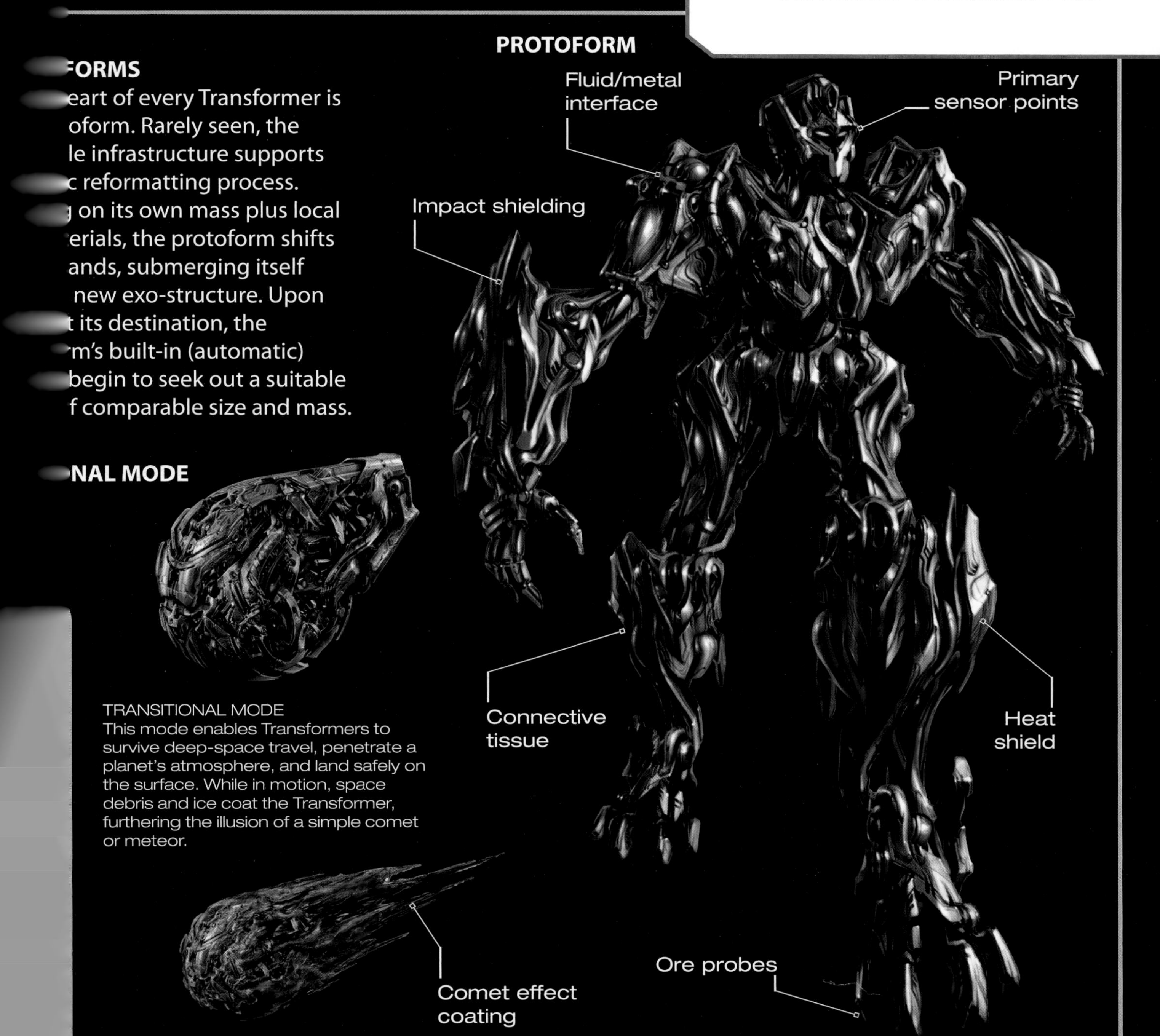

TRANSITIONAL MODE
This mode enables Transformers to survive deep-space travel, penetrate a planet's atmosphere, and land safely on the surface. While in motion, space debris and ice coat the Transformer, furthering the illusion of a simple comet or meteor.

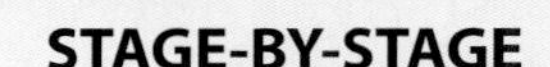

STAGE-BY-STAGE

When Autobot Optimus Prime arrives on Earth, he chooses a disguise that fits his mass and reflects his personality. The first step is location—using a broad-spectrum scan of all local info-feeds, such as the Internet. Next is acquisition—onboard systems create a like for like virtual schematic of the alternative mode. Then comes trans-scanning—a full meta-digital composition of the new form. The final stage is compositing—the drawing together of the necessary extra raw materials.

OPTIMUS PRIME

AUTOBOT LEADER

A WISE AND BENEFICENT leader turned reluctant warrior hero, Optimus Prime spearheads the struggle to protect—at any cost—the sacred Allspark from Megatron's vile ambition and the corruption that seems destined to follow. In peacetime, Prime was a stoic, dignified head of state, ruling with compassion and forbearance. In wartime, despite the heavy toll of countless battles and ever-mounting casualties, those qualities still define his character.

THE GIFT OF LIFE

"Where there is life, there is hope." So said Optimus Prime as he made last-ditch preparations to launch the Allspark into space. Prime knew full well that without the Allspark, Cybertron itself might die. But, somewhere in the vast universe, the Allspark would bring its gift of life to others. For Prime, that was enough.

TECHNICAL DATA

Height: 28'
Weight: 4.3 metric tons
Strength: Power Level 10

X MARKS THE SPOT
Written in the ancient language of the Primes, the map etched on Archibald Witwicky's glasses identifying the final resting place of the Allspark is unintelligible to most. But for Optimus Prime, a descendent of the original Thirteen, it is child's play.

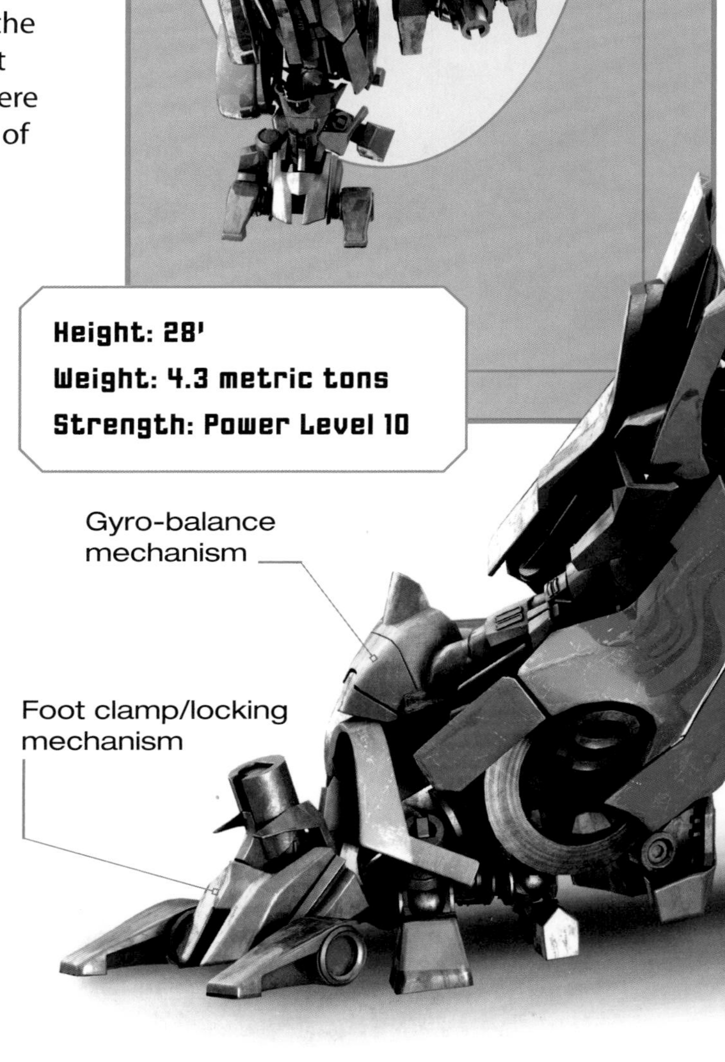

OPTIMUS PRIME
ROBOT MODE

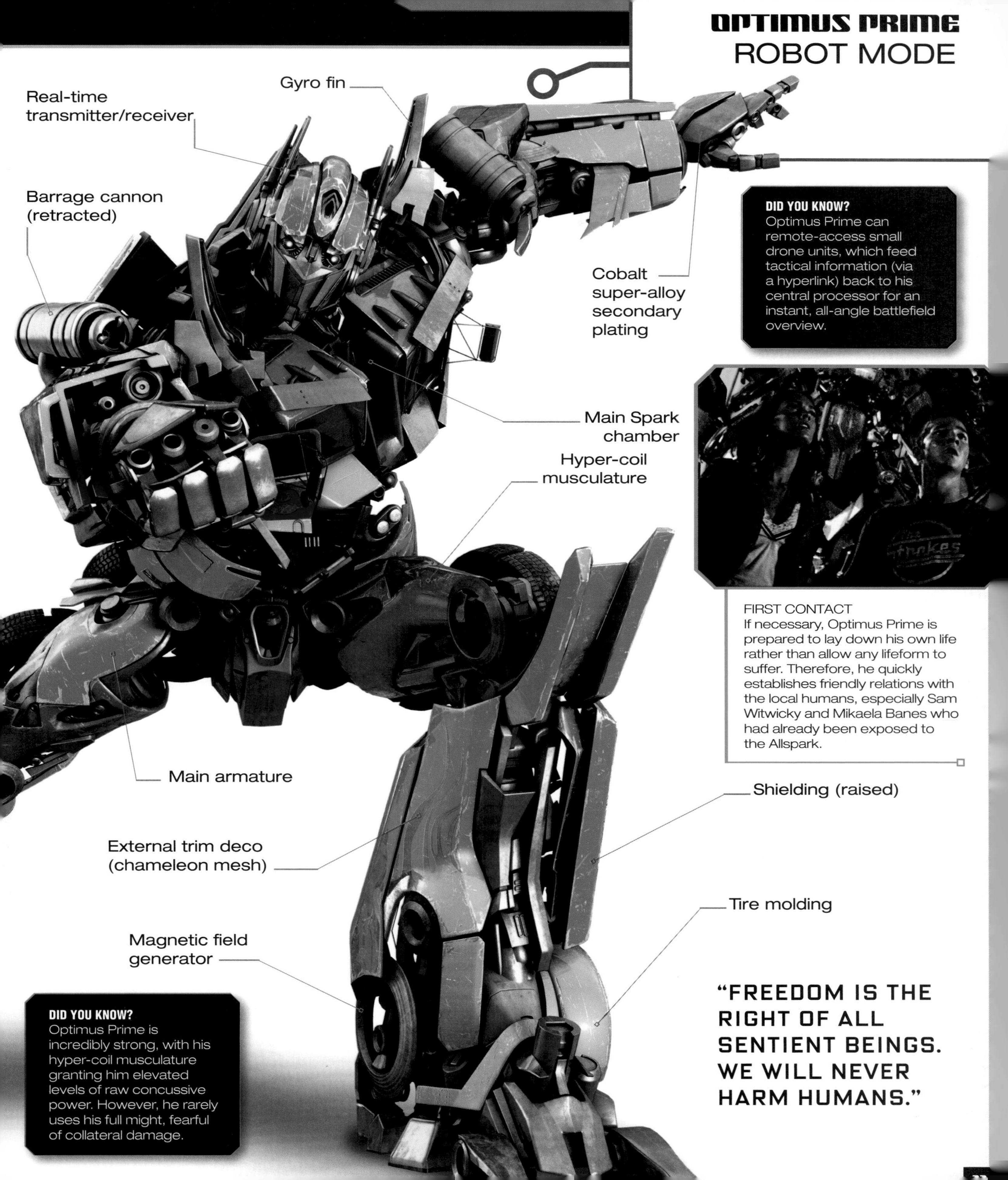

DID YOU KNOW?
Optimus Prime can remote-access small drone units, which feed tactical information (via a hyperlink) back to his central processor for an instant, all-angle battlefield overview.

FIRST CONTACT
If necessary, Optimus Prime is prepared to lay down his own life rather than allow any lifeform to suffer. Therefore, he quickly establishes friendly relations with the local humans, especially Sam Witwicky and Mikaela Banes who had already been exposed to the Allspark.

DID YOU KNOW?
Optimus Prime is incredibly strong, with his hyper-coil musculature granting him elevated levels of raw concussive power. However, he rarely uses his full might, fearful of collateral damage.

"FREEDOM IS THE RIGHT OF ALL SENTIENT BEINGS. WE WILL NEVER HARM HUMANS."

OPTIMUS PRIME

DID YOU KNOW?
Optimus Prime can access extra (reserve) power from compacted energy cells on either flank. These volatile, heavily shielded units are accessed only in extreme emergencies.

KEENLY AWARE THAT he has, albeit inadvertently, brought war to Earth, Optimus Prime sets out to prevent it escalating catastrophically. Before he can do that, Prime needs both mobility and camouflage. In theory, Cybertronian technology allows for the trans-scanning process to work on any given specification, but in truth each robot needs a non-sentient template of roughly the same overall mass. So, when a semi-truck thunders along a nearby highway, Prime has no hesitation in reformatting his body accordingly.

FRONT RUNNER
The toughest enemy siege defenses prove little obstacle to Optimus Prime when he's fully rolling in vehicle mode. In any battle it is Prime who leads the charge, clearing the way for his fellow ground troops. Inspirational, unstoppable, indomitable—Prime leads by example.

TECHNICAL DATA

Top speed: 250 mph
0–60 in: 1.25 seconds
Engine: 850 HP
Max haulage: 600 metric tons

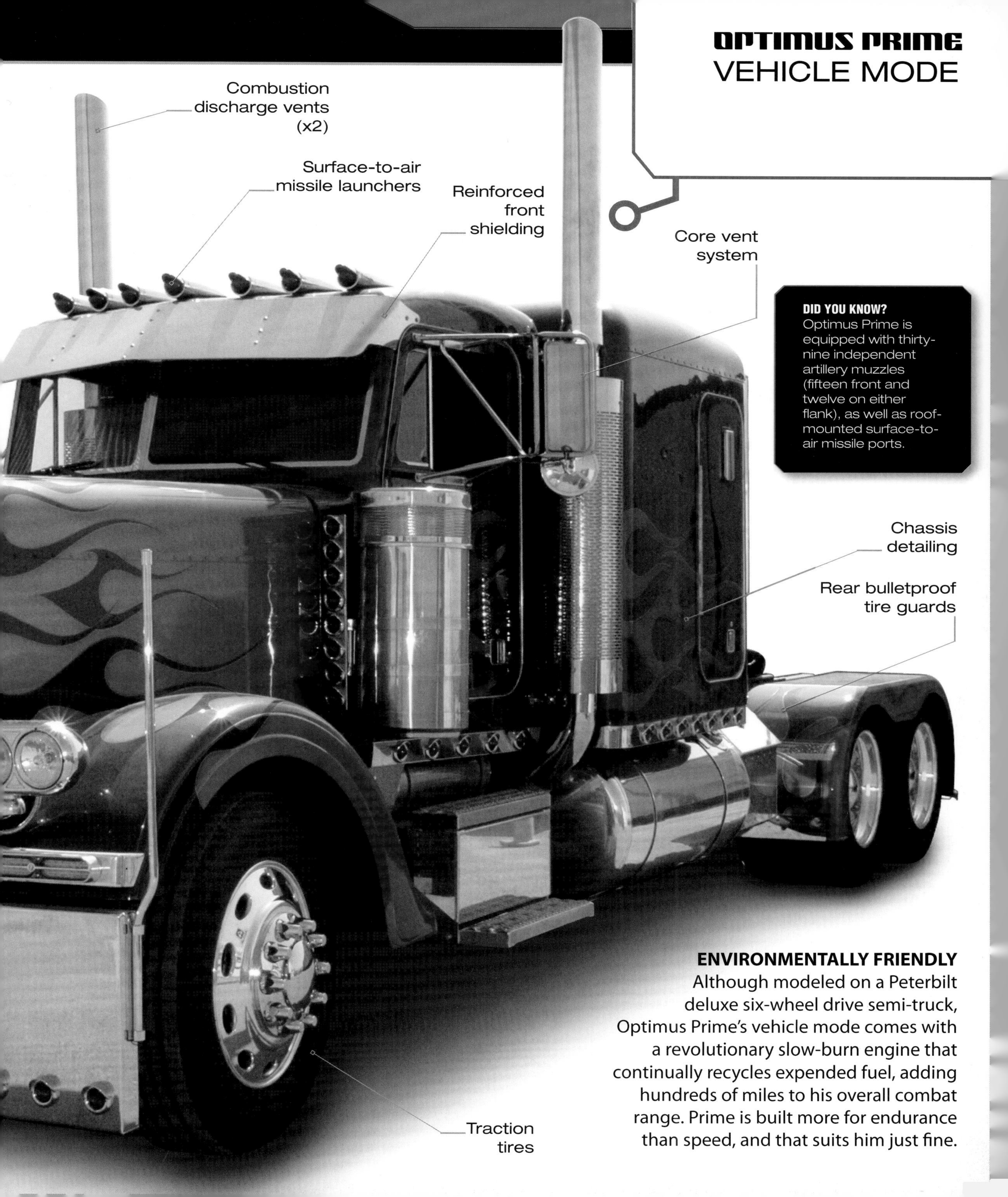

OPTIMUS PRIME VEHICLE MODE

DID YOU KNOW?
Optimus Prime is equipped with thirty-nine independent artillery muzzles (fifteen front and twelve on either flank), as well as roof-mounted surface-to-air missile ports.

ENVIRONMENTALLY FRIENDLY
Although modeled on a Peterbilt deluxe six-wheel drive semi-truck, Optimus Prime's vehicle mode comes with a revolutionary slow-burn engine that continually recycles expended fuel, adding hundreds of miles to his overall combat range. Prime is built more for endurance than speed, and that suits him just fine.

ROAD WARRIOR
On the overcrowded highways of Earth, Optimus Prime knows that the key to any kind of combat is rapid response, as an extended battle would endanger lives. Sure enough, when Prime engages Bonecrusher on an elevated stretch of freeway, he ends the combat with a swift thrust of battle blade.

Insulated blade sheath

Locking catch

Chargeable blade

Non-conductive brace

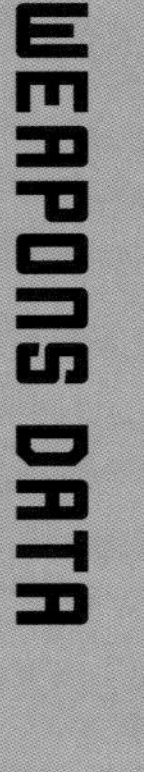

BARRAGE CANNON
Range: 1.2 miles
Max yield: 3 kt
Warhead: Plutonium
Firing rate: 6 per second

BATTLE BLADE
Range: N/A
Max yield: 1,000 degrees C
Energy source: Quantum electric generator
Burn rate: 5 kilojoules per second

MORE OFTEN THAN NOT, Optimus Prime would rather reason his way out of a tight spot, but that doesn't mean he can't, or won't, fight fire with fire. His laser-sighted barrage cannon fires plutonium-tipped warheads up to a range of sixty miles, the explosive force equal to approximately 3,000 lbs of TNT. An auto-reloader and reserve battery allows for "spread" firing. Secondary pulse weapons rapid-fire charged (10 megawatt) energy particles, creating a "firewall" effect.

OPTIMUS PRIME
WEAPON MODE

DID YOU KNOW?
In addition to his barrage cannon, Optimus Prime wields a retractable battle blade. It has a built-in network of microscopic electrical storage cells that allows one section of the blade to be charged up to a surface temperature of 1,000°C. The secondary blade, made of a specially treated non-conductive metal, acts as a sheath, preventing Prime from feeling the effects of his own "live" blade.

MEGATRON
DECEPTICON TYRANT

THE FORMER LORD High Protector of Cybertron, Megatron's ambitions overpowered his once firm but fair nature. In secret, he coveted the Allspark's limitless power for himself. When he had the chance, he struck, brutally and mercilessly, his army swiftly mastering the ways of war. Consumed by sheer lust for power, Megatron soon graduated to greater atrocities, devastating the planet he once served.

DID YOU KNOW?
Megatron is powerful beyond measure, possessing an internal, self-regenerating dark matter power core of possibly alien origin.

TECHNICAL DATA

Height: 35'

Weight: 5.7 metric tons

Strength: Power Level 5

UN-CIVIL DEFENSE
On Cybertron, Megatron came close to securing the Allspark. Determined to possess its life-giving powers, he homed in on the Allspark's unique energy signal. But, when the Allspark was subsequently ejected into space, he was forced to begin his quest anew.

ON ICE!
Relentlessly, Megatron tracked the Allspark to Earth. But his passage through the atmosphere resulted in his super-heated form plunging deep into the Arctic ice. He remained there until discovered by Captain Archibald Witwicky and transferred to the Sector 7 base under the Hoover Dam. There, Megatron was kept in cold storage, cryogenically frozen.

MEGATRON
ROBOT MODE

"I AM THE DESTROYER OF WORLDS."

MEGATRON

DID YOU KNOW?
Megatron's unique configuration in tank mode makes him supremely resistant to harm, his interlocking/layered armored carapace able to withstand even the most intense artillery barrages. Armed with twin plasma cannons and a laser-sighted missile launcher with interchangeable "smart" warheads, Megatron is an unstoppable army of one.

WHILE OTHER TRANSFORMERS opt for a vehicular disguise designed to blend in with their surroundings, Megatron does the opposite. He wants to be recognized instantly to inspire the joint-locking fear that goes hand-in-hand with his name. So, whether it's his terrifying interstellar jet mode or his equally awesome and dread super-tank mode, there's just no mistaking Megatron, and the net result is always the same—sheer devastation and total annihilation.

TRIPLE-CHANGER

Since his "rebirth," Megatron has become relatively unique among Decepticons—a triple-changer. With options such as raining lightning down from his wingtips or crushing and grinding his foes beneath his razor-edged tank tracks, Megatron's arrival heralds doom and despair.

Primary neutronic thrusters

Rear stabiliser fin

Carbonized hull plating

Forward barrage weapons (extended)

Stealth mode field generators

Interstellar slipstream channels

Starboard lightning emitter

JET MODE
Top speed: Mach 3
0–60 in: 0.011 seconds
Engine: Plasma-injection
Lift potential: 2,000 metric tons

TECHNICAL DATA

MEGATRON
VEHICLE MODE

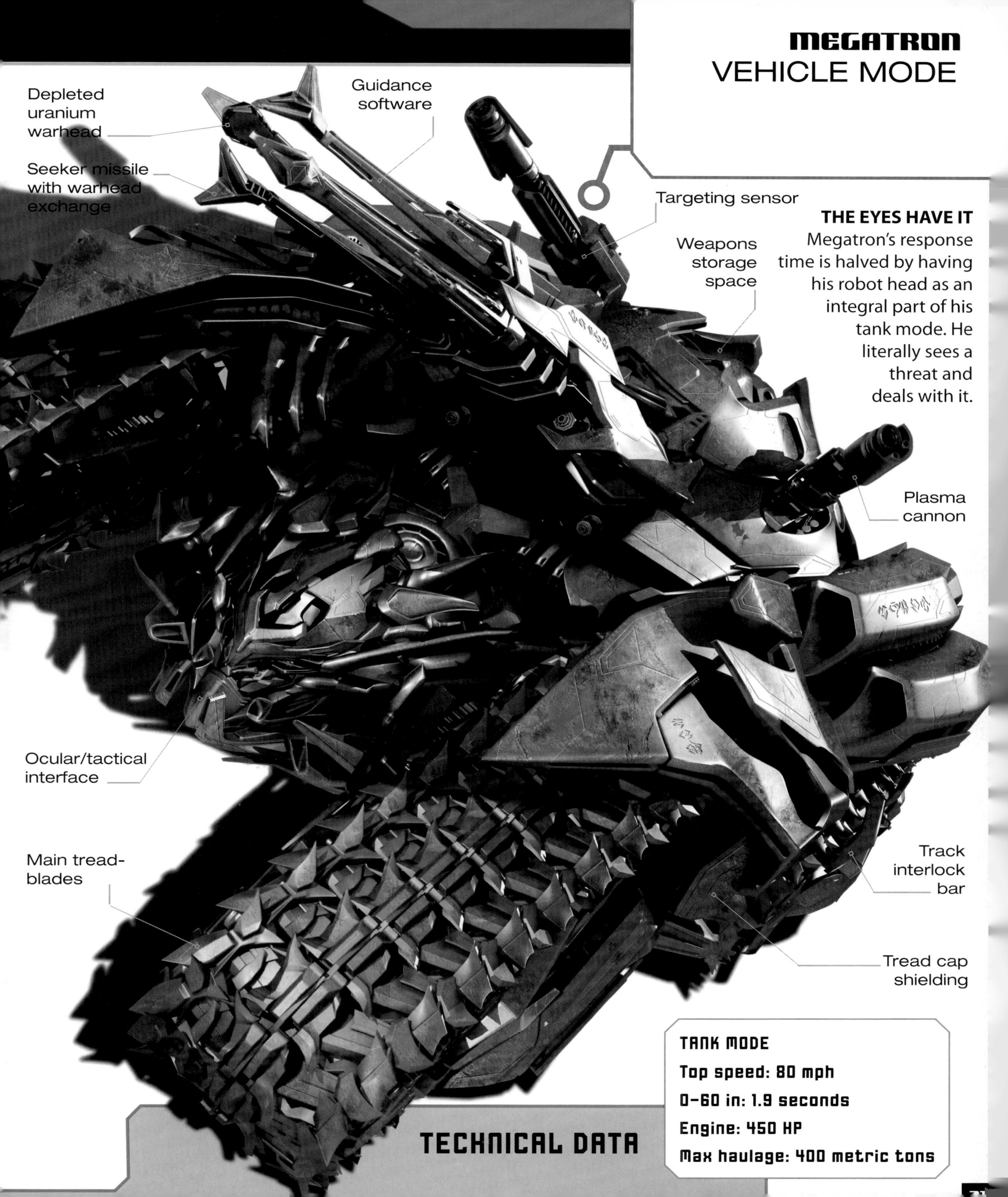

THE EYES HAVE IT
Megatron's response time is halved by having his robot head as an integral part of his tank mode. He literally sees a threat and deals with it.

TECHNICAL DATA

TANK MODE
Top speed: 80 mph
0–60 in: 1.9 seconds
Engine: 450 HP
Max haulage: 400 metric tons

MEGATRON

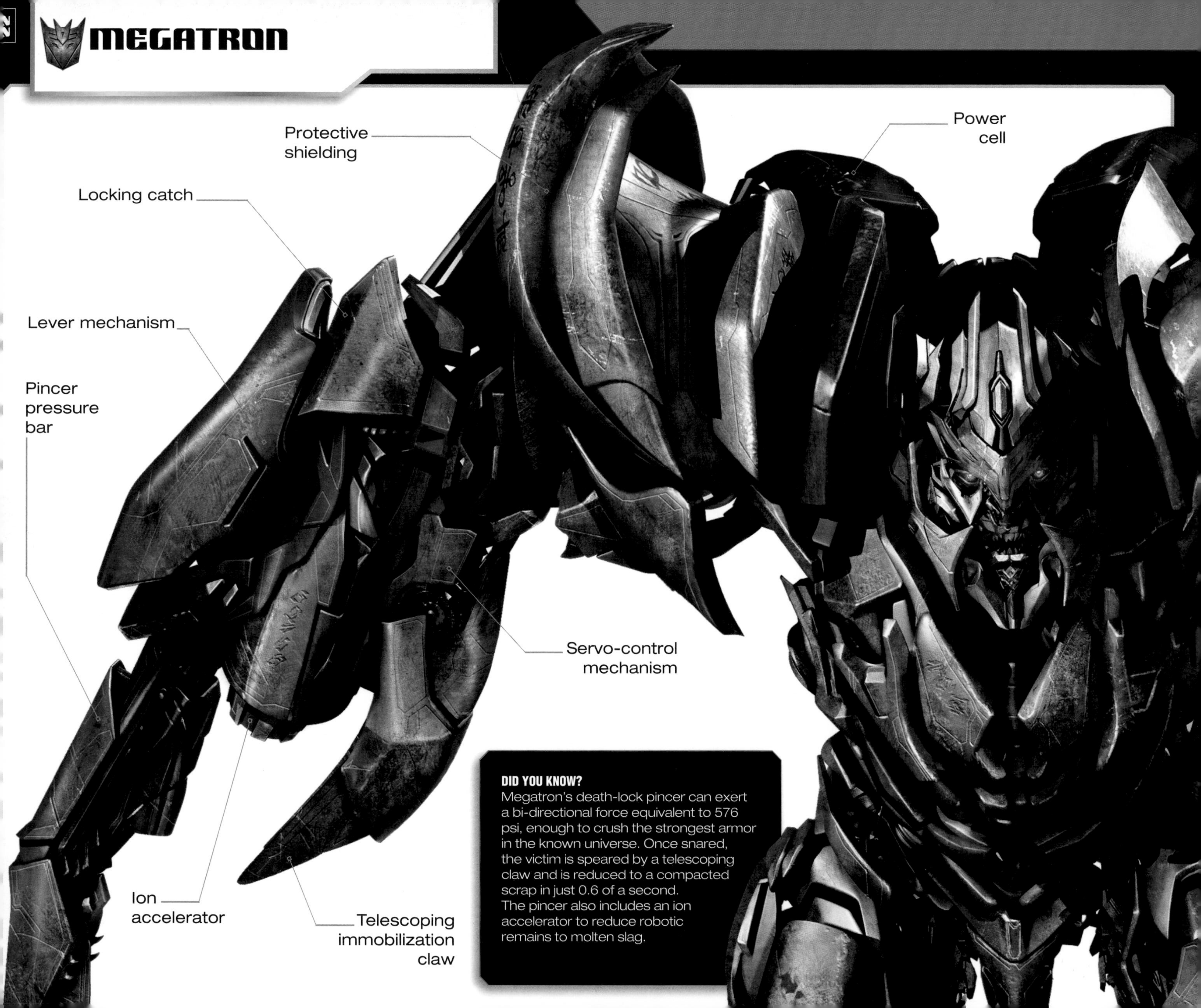

DID YOU KNOW?
Megatron's death-lock pincer can exert a bi-directional force equivalent to 576 psi, enough to crush the strongest armor in the known universe. Once snared, the victim is speared by a telescoping claw and is reduced to a compacted scrap in just 0.6 of a second. The pincer also includes an ion accelerator to reduce robotic remains to molten slag.

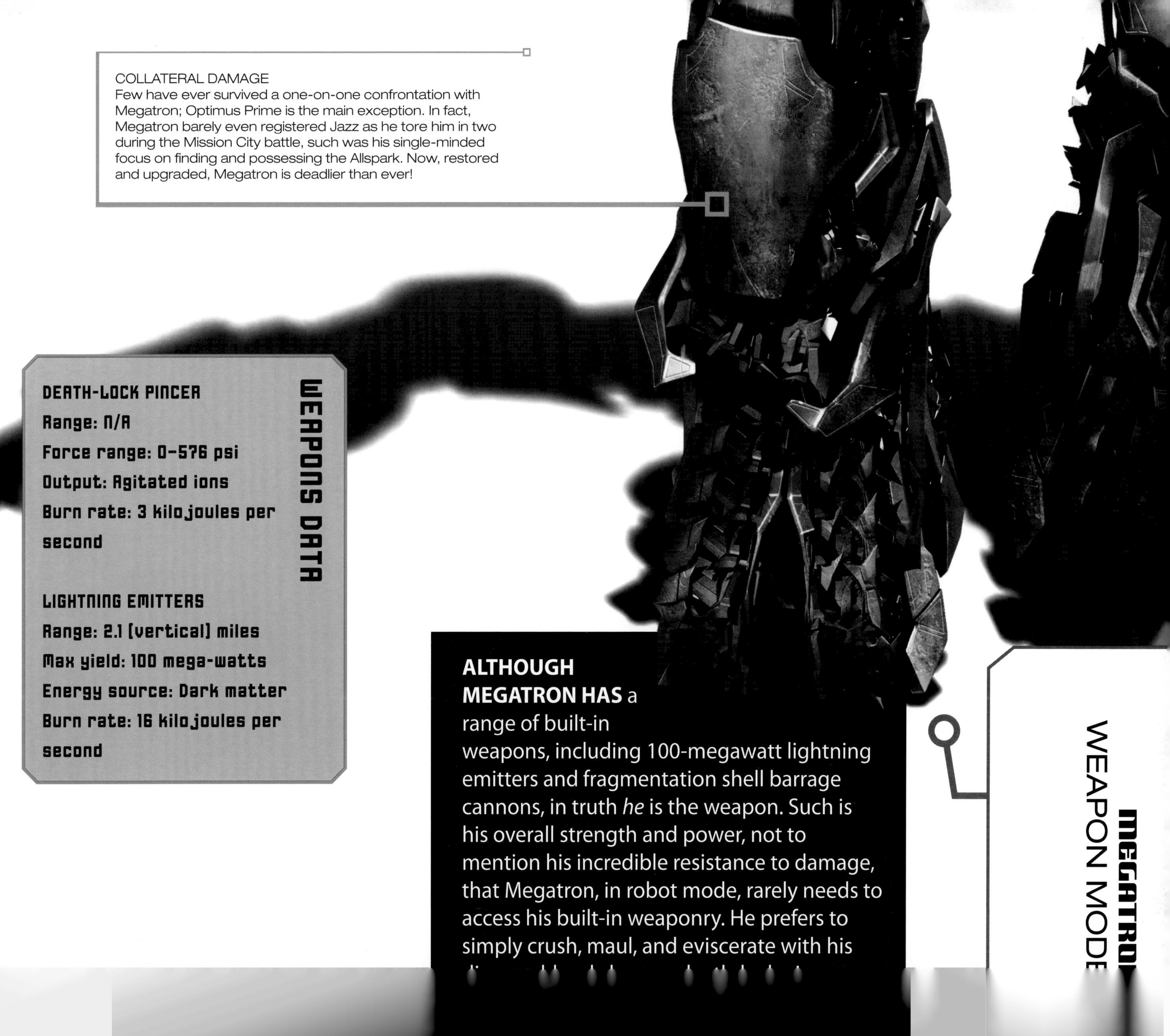

MEGATRO
WEAPON MOD

COLLATERAL DAMAGE
Few have ever survived a one-on-one confrontation with Megatron; Optimus Prime is the main exception. In fact, Megatron barely even registered Jazz as he tore him in two during the Mission City battle, such was his single-minded focus on finding and possessing the Allspark. Now, restored and upgraded, Megatron is deadlier than ever!

WEAPONS DATA

DEATH-LOCK PINCER
Range: N/A
Force range: 0–576 psi
Output: Agitated ions
Burn rate: 3 kilojoules per second

LIGHTNING EMITTERS
Range: 2.1 (vertical) miles
Max yield: 100 mega-watts
Energy source: Dark matter
Burn rate: 16 kilojoules per second

ALTHOUGH MEGATRON HAS a range of built-in weapons, including 100-megawatt lightning emitters and fragmentation shell barrage cannons, in truth *he* is the weapon. Such is his overall strength and power, not to mention his incredible resistance to damage, that Megatron, in robot mode, rarely needs to access his built-in weaponry. He prefers to simply crush, maul, and eviscerate with his

SAM WITWICKY

HAND OF FATE

Perhaps it was chance that led Captain Archibald Witwicky, an intrepid explorer, to uncover Megatron's deep-frozen body under the Arctic ice, or maybe it was fate. Certainly when Captain Witwicky bequeathed his glasses to his descendents, he had no idea that they contained an etching of the final resting place of the Allspark. Years later the glasses came into the possession of Archibald's great-great-grandson, a high school student named Sam, who would become an integral part of the next phase of the war between the Autobots and Decepticons. After a somewhat faltering start, Sam rose to this challenge magnificently, aided and abetted by his human allies. He not only guided the Autobots to the Allspark but also took it upon himself to keep it safe during the Mission City siege. He remains a staunch—if now somewhat distant—ally of the Autobots, but it seems clear to Optimus Prime that Sam's ultimate destiny is still to be resolved.

ENDGAME
When Sam takes over protective custody of the Allspark, he finds reserves of strength he didn't know he possessed. Evading the murderous attentions of both Starscream and Megatron, Sam takes charge of his own destiny, destroying Megatron by thrusting the Allspark deep into the Decepticon's chest cavity.

MIKAELA BANES

The object of Sam's long-range affections, Mikaela Banes is a large part of the reason Sam wants a car (Bumblebee) in the first place, but instead of impressing her, he just manages to endanger her as well. Nevertheless, Mikaela more than proves her own mettle in the battles that follow. Sam learns that Mikaela's father is in jail, serving a sentence for grand theft auto, and that Mikaela herself has a juvenile criminal record. But thanks to Sector 7, Sam manages to secure the release of Mikaela's father and quash Mikaela's conviction. She and Sam remain very close friends.

RON AND JUDY WITWICKY

Sam's parents mean well, but the potentially dangerous concept of "saving the world" is hardly what they envisaged as their son's career choice. Although they are now aware of the Autobots and Sam's links to them, they rather discourage further "active duty." With Sam growing up and leaving home to go to college, Ron and Judy worry about Sam's future safety, but know, deep in their hearts, that they have to let him go. However, finally getting Bumblebee out of their garage goes some way to making up for Sam's departure.

HUMAN ALLIES

THEIR WAR... OUR TROOPS!
Blackout's attack on the SOCCENT Forward Operations Base in Qatar marks the first engagement between the Decepticons and Earth's armed forces. This confrontation rapidly escalates—via a desert storm in Qatar, courtesy of Scorponok—into an all-out battle in Mission City. At the forefront of this internal counteroffensive is Special Forces Captain William Lennox and his small but committed group of officers and men, including Technical Sergeant Julius Epps, Chief Warrant Officer Jorge Figueroa, and Sergeant First Class Patrick Donnelly. Now promoted to Major, Lennox—with Epps as his second-in-command—heads up a highly specialized unit dedicated to the exposure and containment of Decepticon deep cover agents on Earth.

LENNOX
A born leader, William Lennox quickly worked his way up through the ranks at great speed, chalking up battle honors in the Gulf and Afghanistan. His easygoing nature and rough and ready sense of humor inspire trust and respect in those under his command. It is Lennox who gives Sam the self-belief he needs to guide the Allspark safely through a raging warzone.

BRING THE RAIN!
During the desert battle with Scorponok, it becomes apparent that conventional artillery has little effect. So, Lennox advocates the use of armor-piercing, hyper-velocity sabot rounds, fired from the 105 millimeter cannons of an AC-130 Spectre gunship.

SECTOR 7

With its existence known only to a few high-ranking officials in US military intelligence, Sector 7's remit is to seek out, control, or eliminate extraterrestrial threats to planet Earth. Sector 7 alone knows the threat posed by the sentient mechanical beings known as Transformers. In the case of former S7 senior tactical agent Simmons (right), giant robot-hunting runs in the family. To maintain its own stringent levels of internal security, Sector 7 often recruits within the same bloodline. Simmons' father and grandfather both served, as did his great-grandfather, the man who supervised the removal of Megatron from the Arctic ice.

AGENT SIMMONS
After their partial exposure and near destruction of their Hoover Dam base, Secretary of State for Defense John Keller disbands S7. But Agent Simmons remains thoroughly attuned to the giant alien robot comings and goings on Earth, though now as a civilian.

NATIONAL SECURITY
Initially, Sector 7 seeks to contain stories of giant robots at large on Earth. They take Sam and Mikaela into protective custody, but the Autobots intercept the Sector 7 convoy and liberate them. As the crisis escalates, Sector 7—if a little grudgingly—is forced to reassess its position, finally accepting that it, Sam, and the Autobots are all on the same side.

BUMBLEBEE

AUTOBOT SCOUT

A STRONG AND ABIDING sense of duty directs the actions of this tenacious and resourceful Autobot. Bumblebee doesn't want glory or accolades, he just needs to know he got the job done and done well. However, sometimes following orders to the letter conflicts with Bumblebee's deep well of compassion. In his capacity as a tactical ops unit leader, Bumblebee deeply regrets any loss of life, even if it is for the "greater good."

"ACTIONS SPEAK LOUDER THAN WORDS."

ON THE RIGHT TRACK

Bumblebee was one of the first Transformers to reach Earth, having tracked the Allspark across the cosmos. The trail led to Archibald Witwicky's great-great-grandson, Sam. Posing as Sam's first car, Bumblebee bonded with the teen. He remains fiercely protective of him, to the extent that Sam is rarely left on his own.

TECHNICAL DATA

Height: 16' 2"

Weight: 1.6 metric tons

Strength: Power Level 2

SILENT PROTECTOR
In the pivotal Cybertronian battle of Tyger Pax, as the Allspark lies within Megatron's grasp, Bumblebee throws himself into a battle he can't possibly win. Already critically injured, Bumblebee is rendered mute when Megatron crushes his vocal processor.

BUMBLEBEE
ROBOT MODE

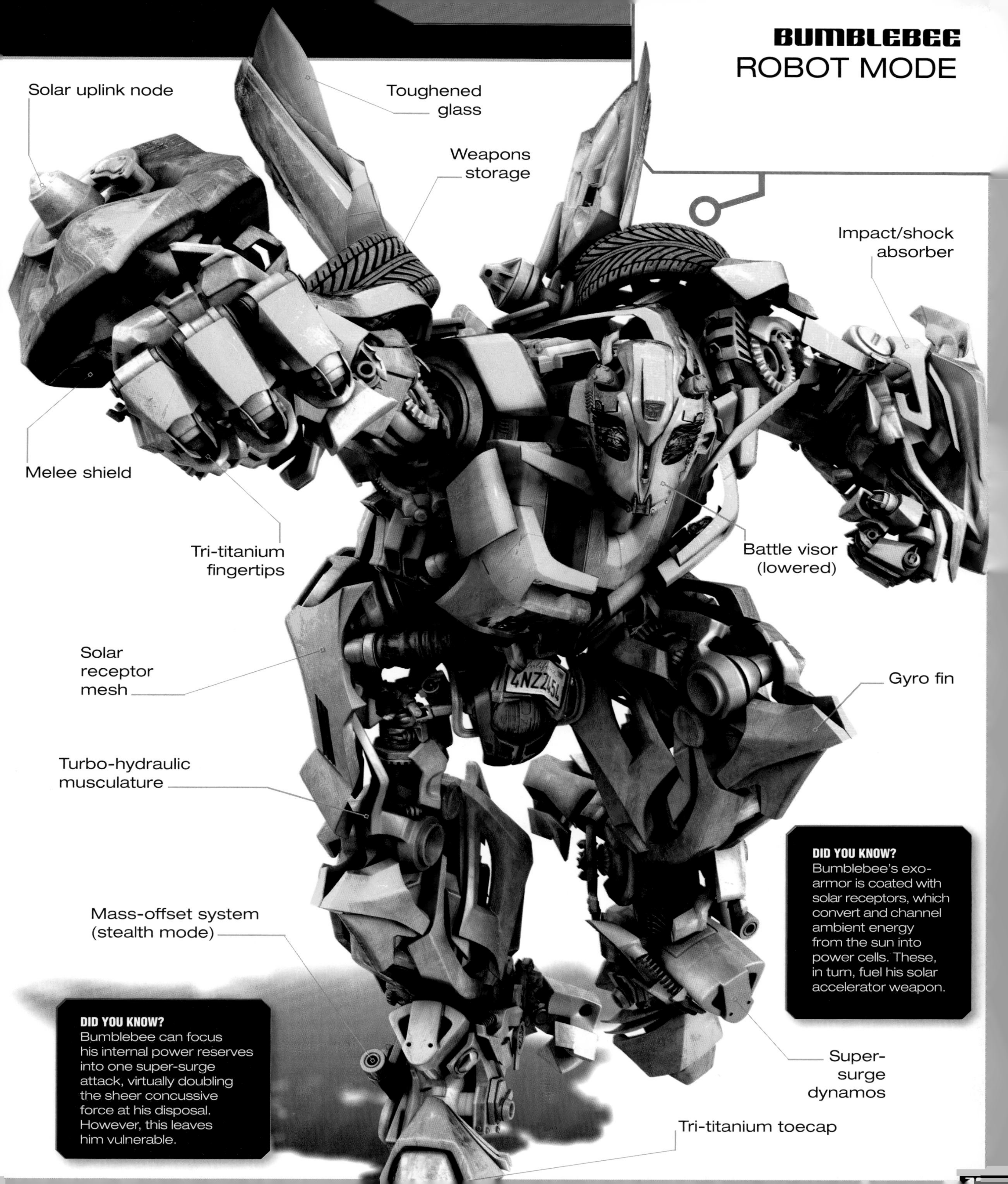

DID YOU KNOW?
Bumblebee's exo-armor is coated with solar receptors, which convert and channel ambient energy from the sun into power cells. These, in turn, fuel his solar accelerator weapon.

DID YOU KNOW?
Bumblebee can focus his internal power reserves into one super-surge attack, virtually doubling the sheer concussive force at his disposal. However, this leaves him vulnerable.

BUMBLEBEE

NEVER ONE TO STAND out in a crowd, Bumblebee's sheer lack of vanity means that when first selecting an Earth disguise he doesn't consider that there might be better, newer options. The beaten-up classic Camaro he trans-scans seems adequate, and Bumblebee takes its limitations in his stride. As it turns out, the selection proves ideal, as it gives Bumblebee the perfect cover in Bobby Bolivia's used car lot.

DID YOU KNOW?
Bumblebee specialises in hit-and-run tactics, using his evasive skills to get in range and then his extensive inbuilt artillery (concussive "flash" shells) to fell his target.

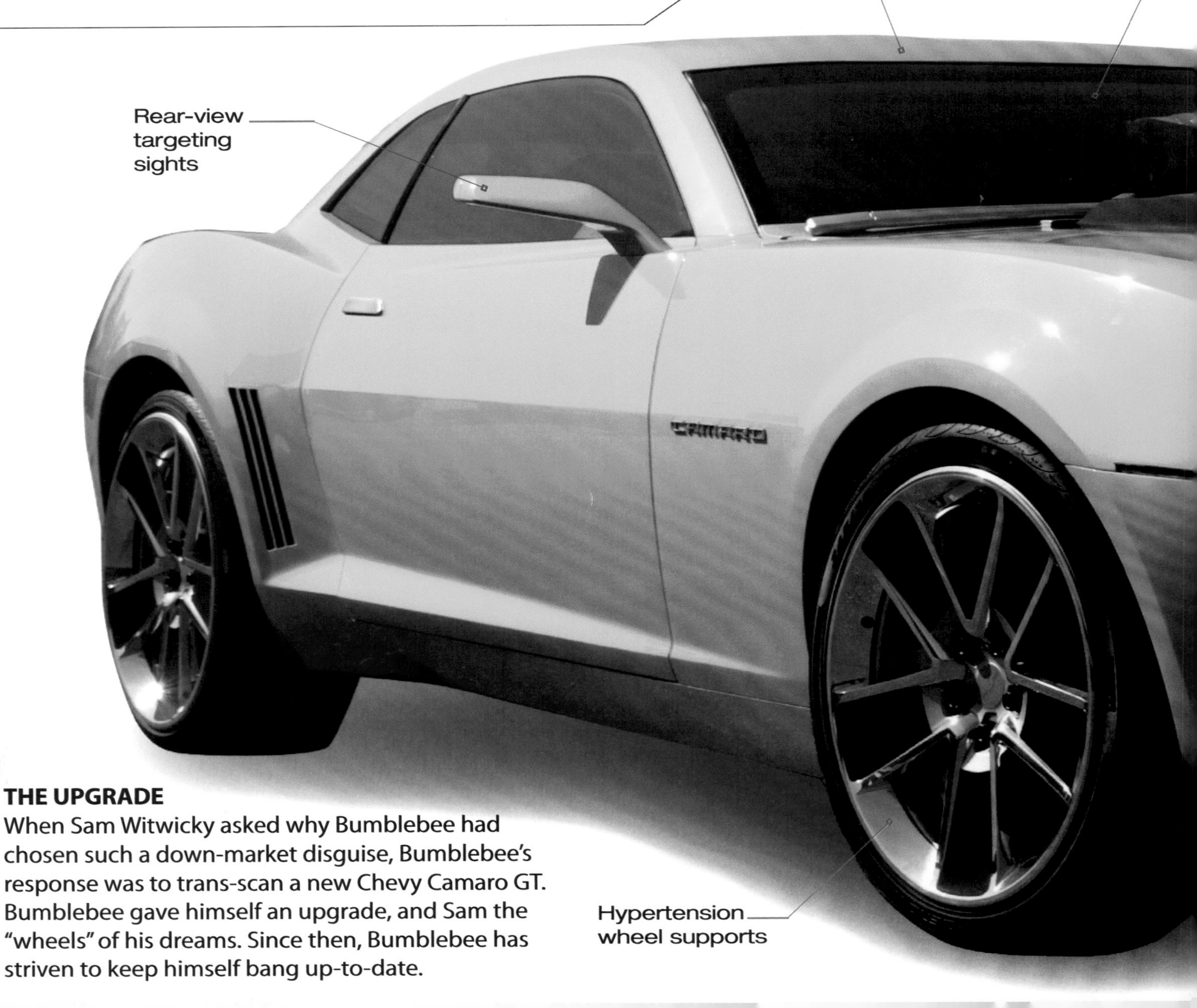

THE UPGRADE
When Sam Witwicky asked why Bumblebee had chosen such a down-market disguise, Bumblebee's response was to trans-scan a new Chevy Camaro GT. Bumblebee gave himself an upgrade, and Sam the "wheels" of his dreams. Since then, Bumblebee has striven to keep himself bang up-to-date.

BUMBLEBEE
VEHICLE MODE

BUYING BUMBLEBEE
It may never be known whether Bumblebee intended for Sam to buy him from Bobby Bolivia's used car lot, or it was simply that they were both in the right place at the right time. In any case, for Sam it is the beginning of the great adventure he has always sought.

TECHNICAL DATA

Top speed: 230 mph
0–60 in: 0.96 seconds
Engine: 450 HP
Max haulage: 50 metric tons

Main armaments cover

Trans-scanning image intensifier

Seeker missile port

Range-finder sensor web

DID YOU KNOW?
Bumblebee's solar receptors can be turned into emitters in vehicle mode, generating a chassis-wide burst of sensor-overloading brilliance that can render surveillance cameras useless.

DID YOU KNOW?
Bumblebee's new mortar delivery system has its share of high explosive charges, but this warrior has more than one trick up his carbonized steel sleeve. Among his arsenal are sensory-overloading flash bombs, corrosive gas grenades, incendiary mortars, sticky bombs, and seismic charges. The delivery system is hard-wired into Bumblebee's neural interface, so he selects and fires at the speed of thought.

WEAPONS DATA

MAGNETIC FIELD GENERATOR

Range: 0.1 miles

Output range: 3 kilohertz

Energy source: Solar

Reverse force: 500 psi

MORTAR DELIVERY SYSTEM

Range: 0.4 miles

Warheads: Various

Energy source: Solar

Propulsion: Rocket

BUMBLEBEE WEAPON MODE

Warhead selector

STING LIKE A BEE
For all Bumblebee's new armaments, his greatest weapon remains his natural stealth. His speciality is getting close enough to reach out and touch an opponent without them even knowing he's there. But once he's within range—watch out! Despite Bumblebee's somewhat diminutive size he is a warrior of great resource, speed, and skill, not to mention a decidedly savage streak, especially when his friends are threatened.

AFTER SOME ROUGH TREATMENT, a complete upgrade for Bumblebee was the order of the day, and that refit—courtesy of Ratchet—extended to his weapons systems. Gone was Bumblebee's solar accelerator weapon and in its place a neat balance of defensive and offensive options: a reverse-flux magnetic field generator shield that can deflect most incoming fire and a pair of ten-shot mortar delivery systems with a wide range of payload selections.

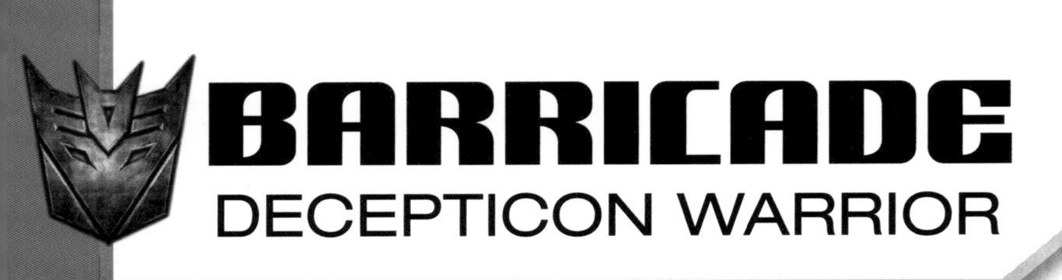

BARRICADE
DECEPTICON WARRIOR

FORGET "PROTECT AND SERVE," Barricade's style is more "maul and batter." This fast, furious Decepticon shock-trooper has a quick temper and an unquenchable thirst for battle. Always at the forefront of any hostile action, Barricade has made himself something of an indispensable tool for Megatron, a fact that doesn't sit well with the ever-ambitious Starscream. Barricade doesn't care, he'll take on anyone… friend or foe!

DID YOU KNOW?
Barricade can probe for weaknesses in defenses or an opponent's armature by switching between analytical, tactical, chemical, and elemental fields of vision.

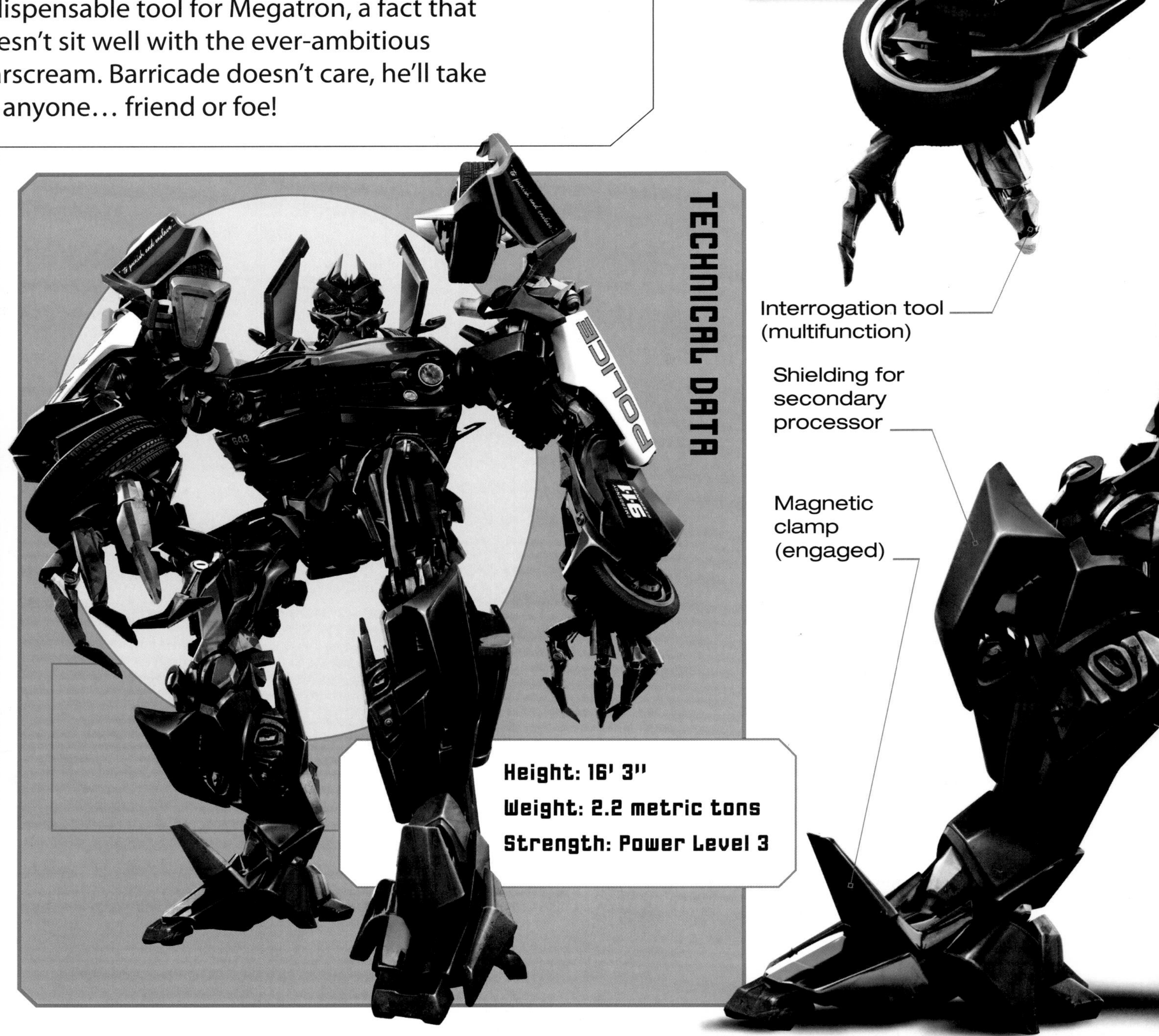

TECHNICAL DATA

Height: 16' 3"

Weight: 2.2 metric tons

Strength: Power Level 3

BARRICADE
ROBOT MODE

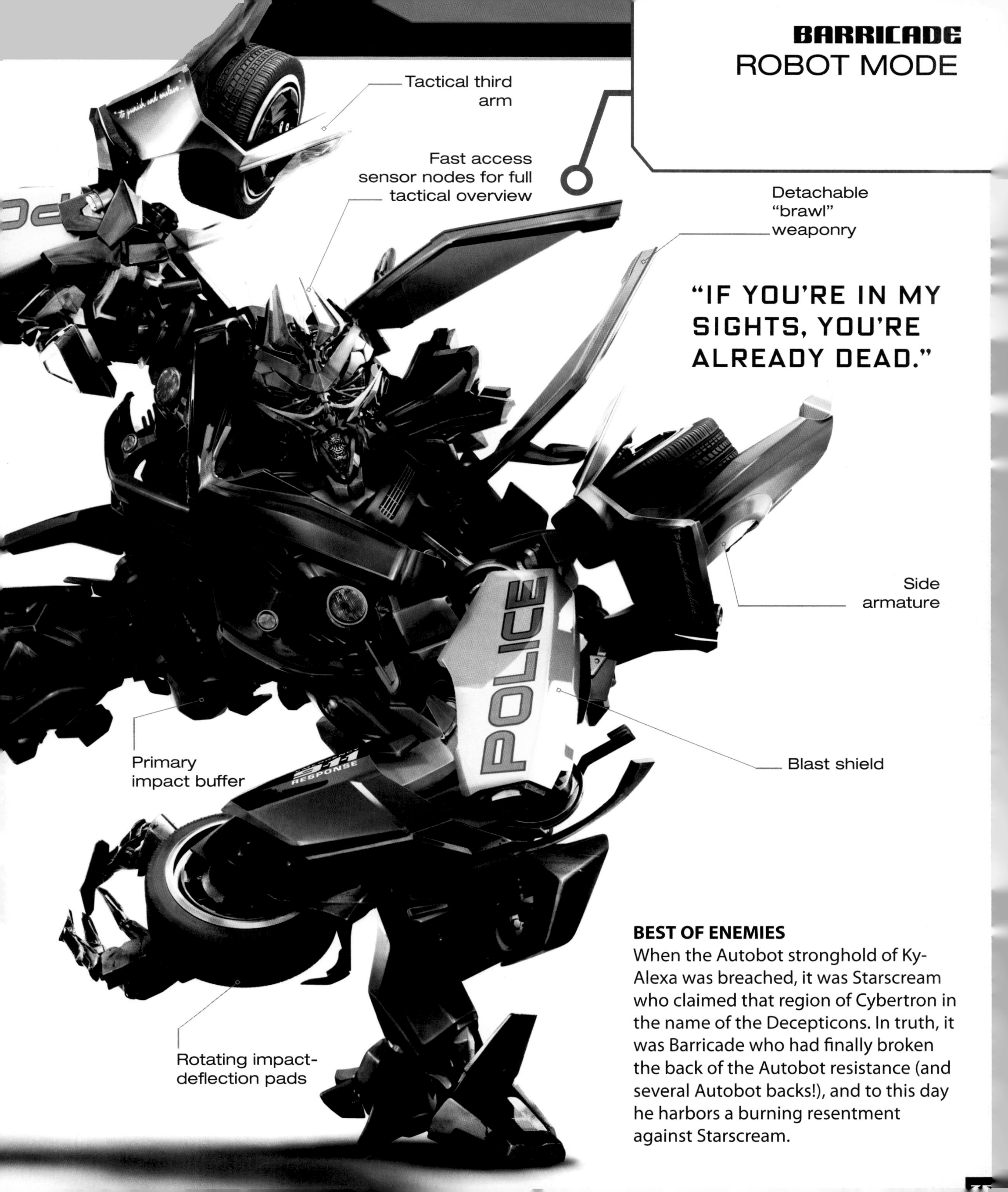

"IF YOU'RE IN MY SIGHTS, YOU'RE ALREADY DEAD."

BEST OF ENEMIES

When the Autobot stronghold of Ky-Alexa was breached, it was Starscream who claimed that region of Cybertron in the name of the Decepticons. In truth, it was Barricade who had finally broken the back of the Autobot resistance (and several Autobot backs!), and to this day he harbors a burning resentment against Starscream.

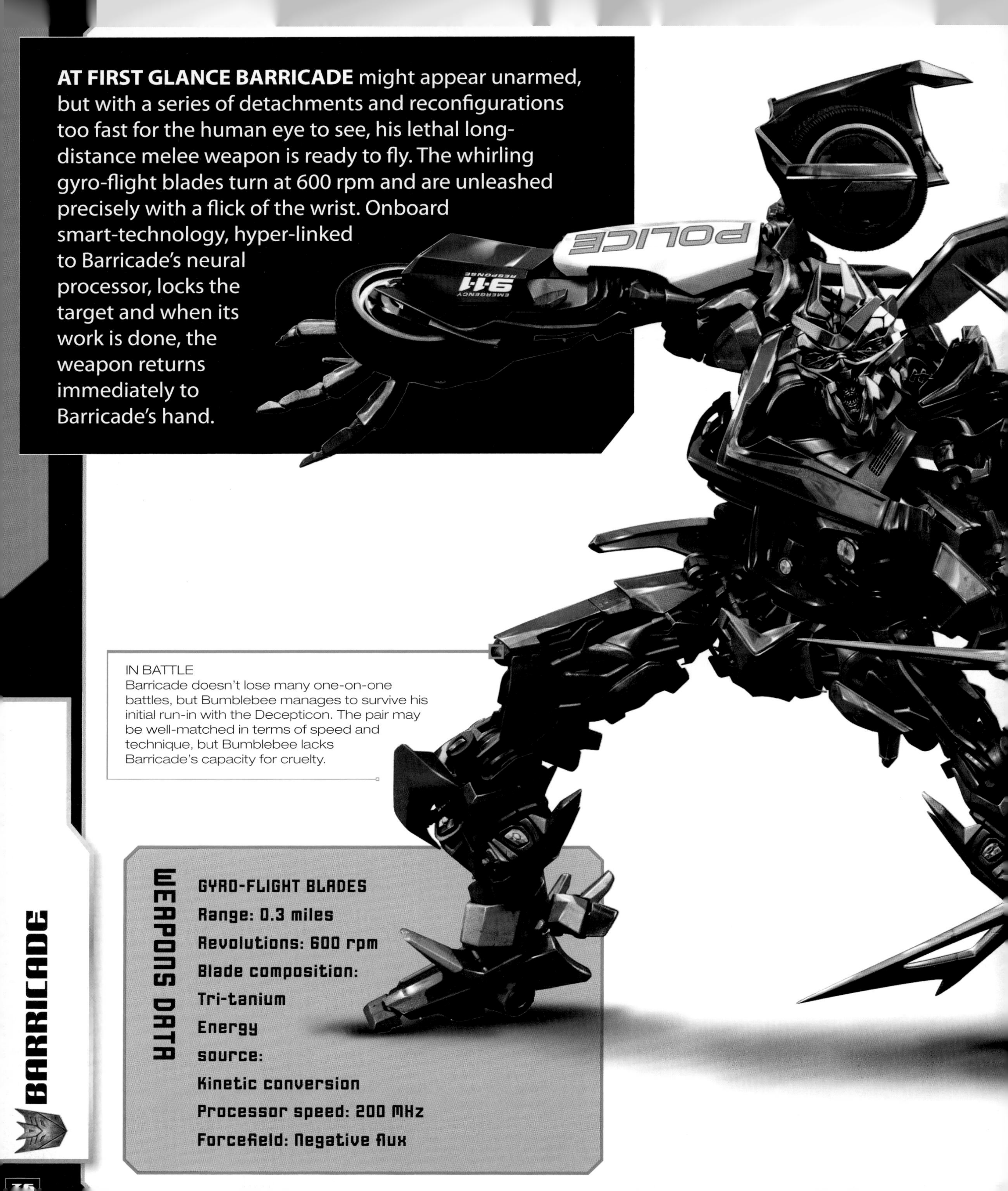

AT FIRST GLANCE BARRICADE might appear unarmed, but with a series of detachments and reconfigurations too fast for the human eye to see, his lethal long-distance melee weapon is ready to fly. The whirling gyro-flight blades turn at 600 rpm and are unleashed precisely with a flick of the wrist. Onboard smart-technology, hyper-linked to Barricade's neural processor, locks the target and when its work is done, the weapon returns immediately to Barricade's hand.

IN BATTLE
Barricade doesn't lose many one-on-one battles, but Bumblebee manages to survive his initial run-in with the Decepticon. The pair may be well-matched in terms of speed and technique, but Bumblebee lacks Barricade's capacity for cruelty.

WEAPONS DATA

GYRO-FLIGHT BLADES
Range: 0.3 miles
Revolutions: 600 rpm
Blade composition: Tri-tanium
Energy source: Kinetic conversion
Processor speed: 200 MHz
Forcefield: Negative flux

BARRICAD
WEAPON MOD

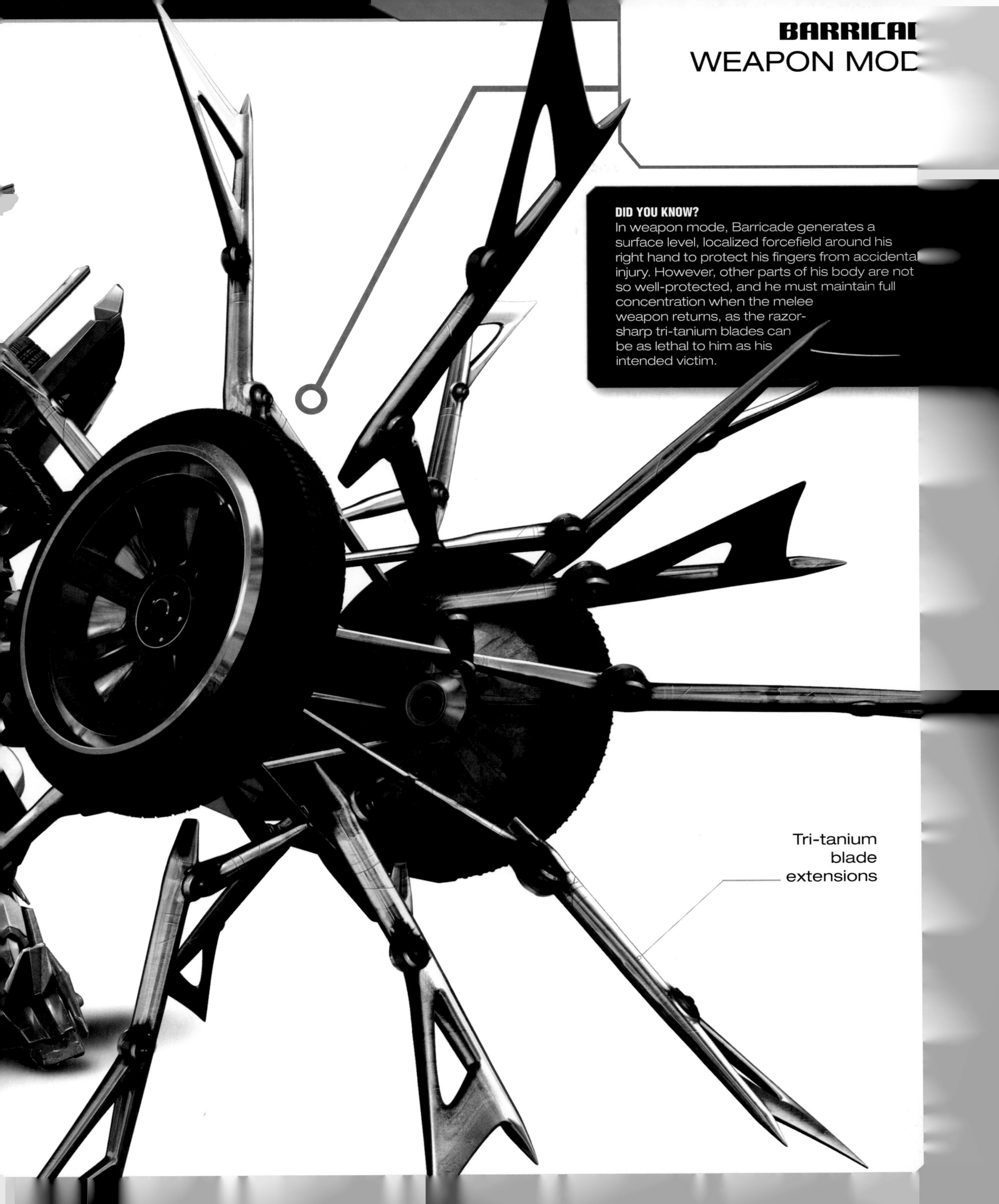

DID YOU KNOW?
In weapon mode, Barricade generates a surface level, localized forcefield around his right hand to protect his fingers from accidenta injury. However, other parts of his body are not so well-protected, and he must maintain full concentration when the melee weapon returns, as the razor-sharp tri-tanium blades can be as lethal to him as his intended victim.

FRENZY
DECEPTICON DEEP COVER AGENT

IN THE CASE OF FRENZY, actions really do speak louder than words. This diminutive but lethal 'bot doesn't say much, but he never, ever gives up or even falters for a second as he carries out subversive infiltration and deep cover missions. Frenzy changes disguises as often as humans change their socks, and he's prepared to dig deep for as long as it takes to get the information he needs.

Retractable dual directional viewpoint

Sensor/probe mandibles

Data-port jacks (multi-access)

Laser cutter

TECHNICAL DATA

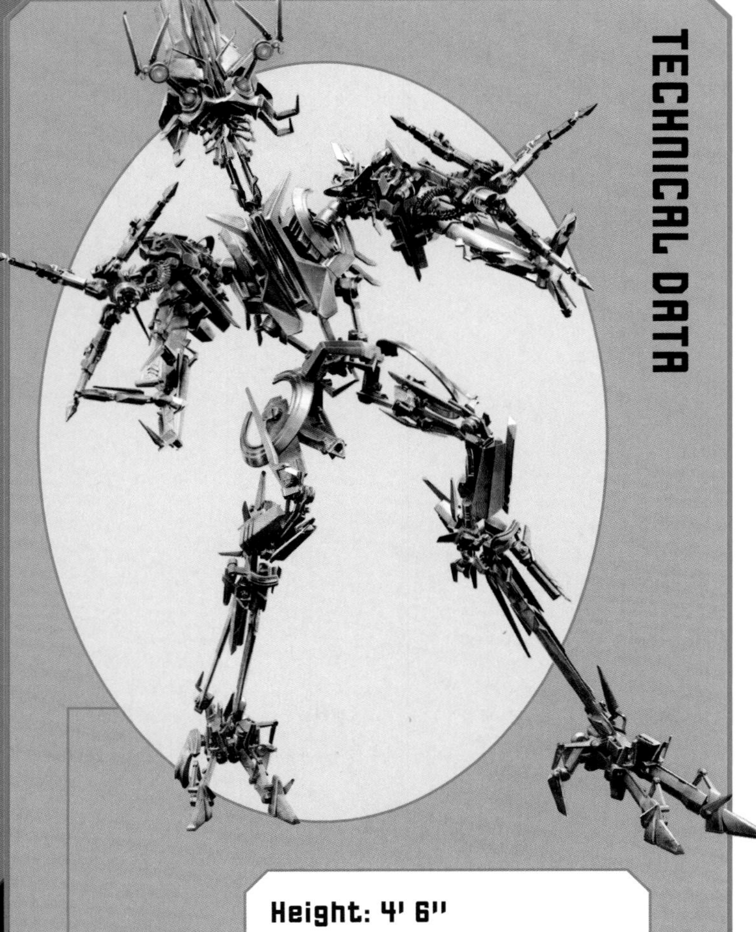

Height: 4' 6''

Weight: 110 kg

Strength: Power Level 1

QUICK-CHANGE

On Earth, Frenzy finds numerous appliances that suit his multi-transforming abilities. Initially, he adopts the disguise of a portable boom box, in order to sneak aboard Air Force One and hack into the Pentagon mainframe for clues to the whereabouts of Megatron.

FRENZY
ROBOT MODE

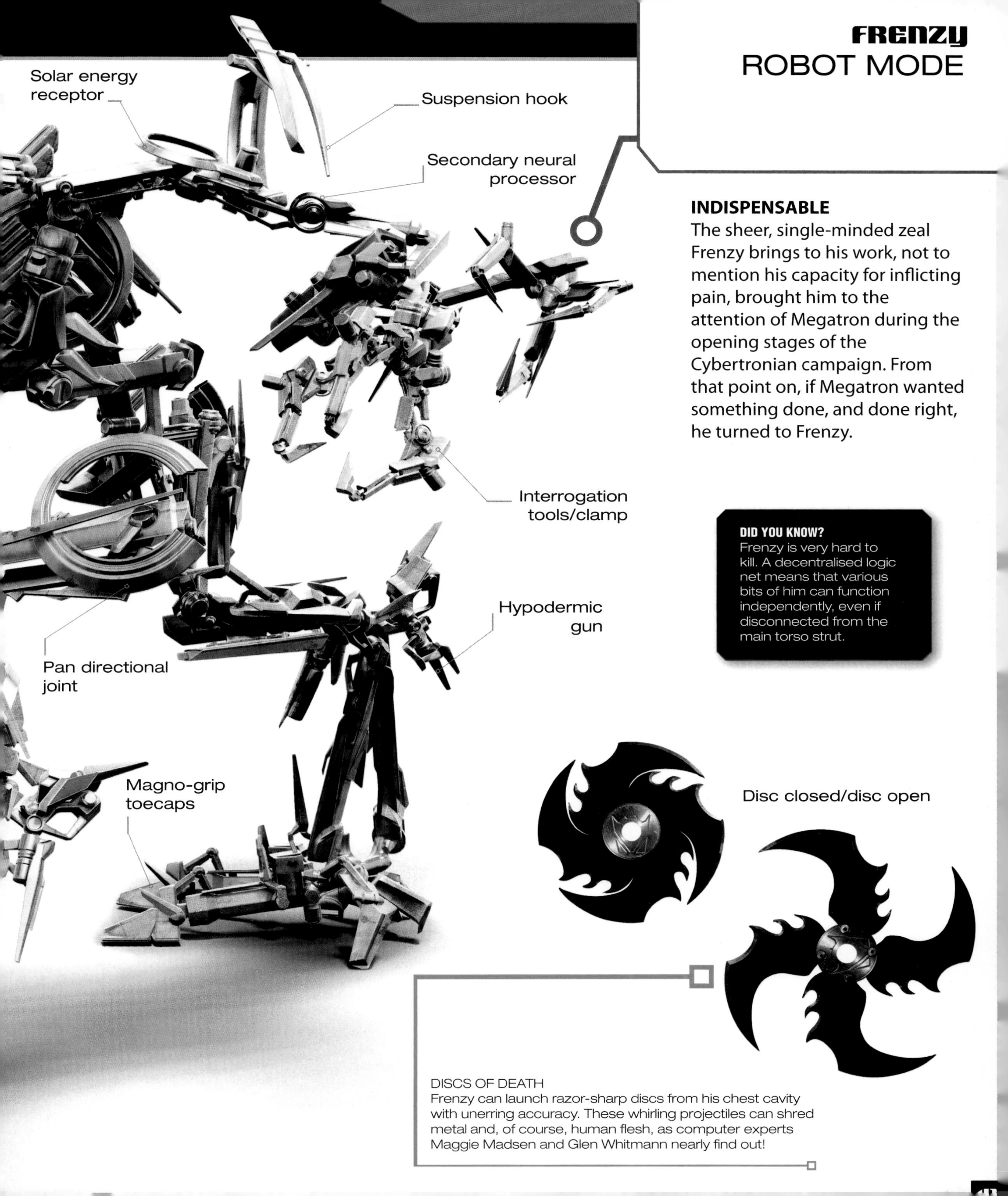

INDISPENSABLE
The sheer, single-minded zeal Frenzy brings to his work, not to mention his capacity for inflicting pain, brought him to the attention of Megatron during the opening stages of the Cybertronian campaign. From that point on, if Megatron wanted something done, and done right, he turned to Frenzy.

DID YOU KNOW?
Frenzy is very hard to kill. A decentralised logic net means that various bits of him can function independently, even if disconnected from the main torso strut.

DISCS OF DEATH
Frenzy can launch razor-sharp discs from his chest cavity with unerring accuracy. These whirling projectiles can shred metal and, of course, human flesh, as computer experts Maggie Madsen and Glen Whitmann nearly find out!

BLACKOUT
DECEPTICON AIR SUPPORT

A SPECIALIST IN SOWING CHAOS, confusion, and disorder, Blackout is a coward at heart. Rather than directly confront an enemy, he will create just enough in the way of general pandemonium to distract and otherwise engage the attention of his intended target before striking (often from behind). Self-preservation is uppermost in his thoughts, and he's not above sacrificing fellow Decepticons if it means he emerges unscathed and intact.

INVASIVE MANEUVERS
Blackout draws first blood in the war on Earth when he attacks the SOCCENT Forward Operations Base in Qatar. Above all he seeks information, and thanks to his uplink tentacles he nearly gets all he needs from the base's mainframe.

Rotor blades

BEHIND ENEMY LINES
On Cybertron, Blackout found himself at the forefront of advance raiding parties, his role being to destabilize Autobot early warning systems and defences. This was at odds with Blackout's usual modus operandi, so he took to enlisting and training his own specialist drone troopers, effectively as a living shield.

Height: 33' 5"
Weight: 2.9 metric tons
Strength: Power Level 2

TECHNICAL DATA

DID YOU KNOW?
Blackout is one of the more lightly armored Decepticons and therefore most liable to sustain critical damage. To protect himself, he maintains a personal air vortex, strong enough to deflect incoming fire.

Scraper probes

BLACKOUT
ROBOT MODE

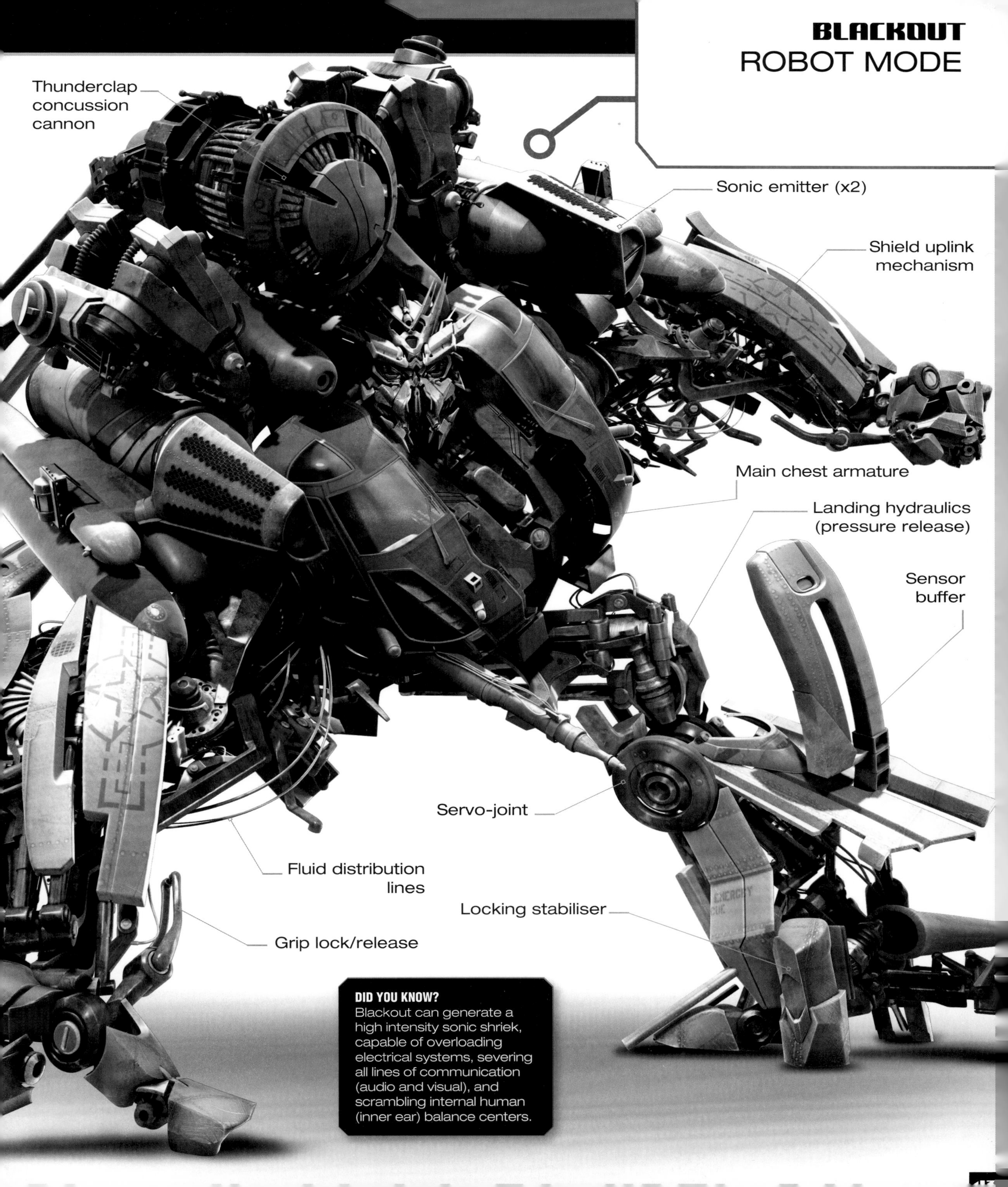

DID YOU KNOW?
Blackout can generate a high intensity sonic shriek, capable of overloading electrical systems, severing all lines of communication (audio and visual), and scrambling internal human (inner ear) balance centers.

ALTHOUGH HE PROBABLY wished otherwise, Blackout was part of the Decepticon unit who arrived on Earth, via Mars, in search of the Allspark and Megatron. In 2003, he was responsible for the destruction of the Beagle Martian rover vehicle, as it surveyed and recorded the Martian landscape. Shortly after on Earth, he came into conflict with Sector 7 tactical units in the New Mexico desert. However, in the Mission City firefight, his lack of heavy armor shielding allowed Major Lennox's mortar strike to lay him low.

DID YOU KNOW?
Blackout can fly in all weather conditions, even practically zero-visibility. Whereas gale-force winds would ground most actual MH-53s, Blackout thrives in such conditions.

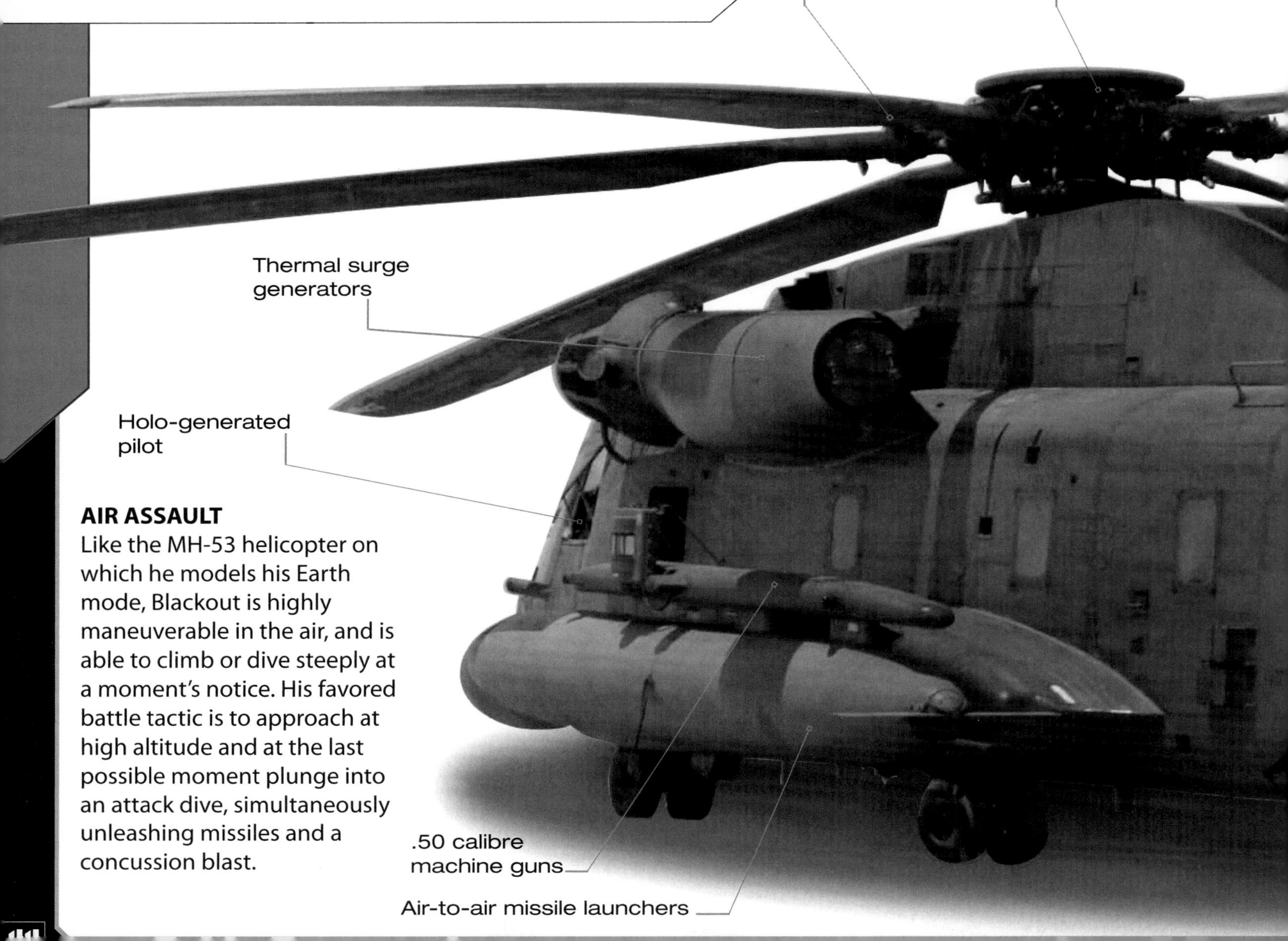

AIR ASSAULT
Like the MH-53 helicopter on which he models his Earth mode, Blackout is highly maneuverable in the air, and is able to climb or dive steeply at a moment's notice. His favored battle tactic is to approach at high altitude and at the last possible moment plunge into an attack dive, simultaneously unleashing missiles and a concussion blast.

BLACKOUT
VEHICLE MODE

TECHNICAL DATA

Top speed: 800 mph
0–60 in: 0.2 seconds
Engine: 7,000 shp (x2)
Lift potential: 650 metric tons

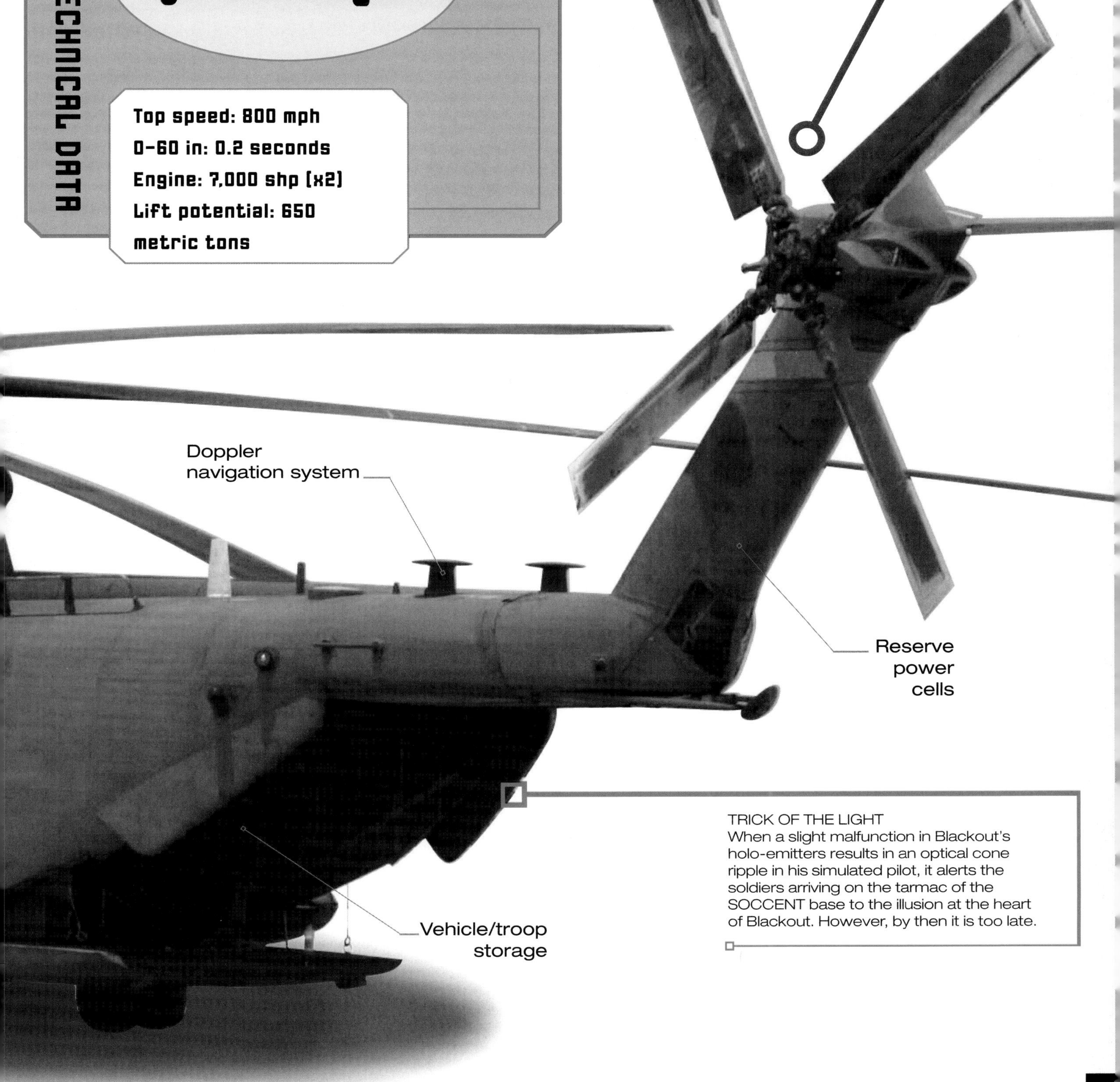

Doppler navigation system

Reserve power cells

Vehicle/troop storage

TRICK OF THE LIGHT
When a slight malfunction in Blackout's holo-emitters results in an optical cone ripple in his simulated pilot, it alerts the soldiers arriving on the tarmac of the SOCCENT base to the illusion at the heart of Blackout. However, by then it is too late.

GIVEN BLACKOUT'S instinct for self-preservation, he favors the more long-distance of his two offensive options. The rotor-blaster, which fits snugly over his left hand, is both a barrage and a melee weapon. For distance destabilization or even immobilization the Thunderclap concussion cannon comes into its own, emitting a 700-decibel sonic shockwave. A directional vortex created by the simultaneously whirling blades guides it to the target with focus and accuracy.

WEAPONS DATA

ROTOR BLASTER
Range: 2.9 miles
Revolutions: 6,000 rpm
Blade composition: Toughened cobalt
Energy source: Updraft dynamo
Sound output (max): 700 decibels

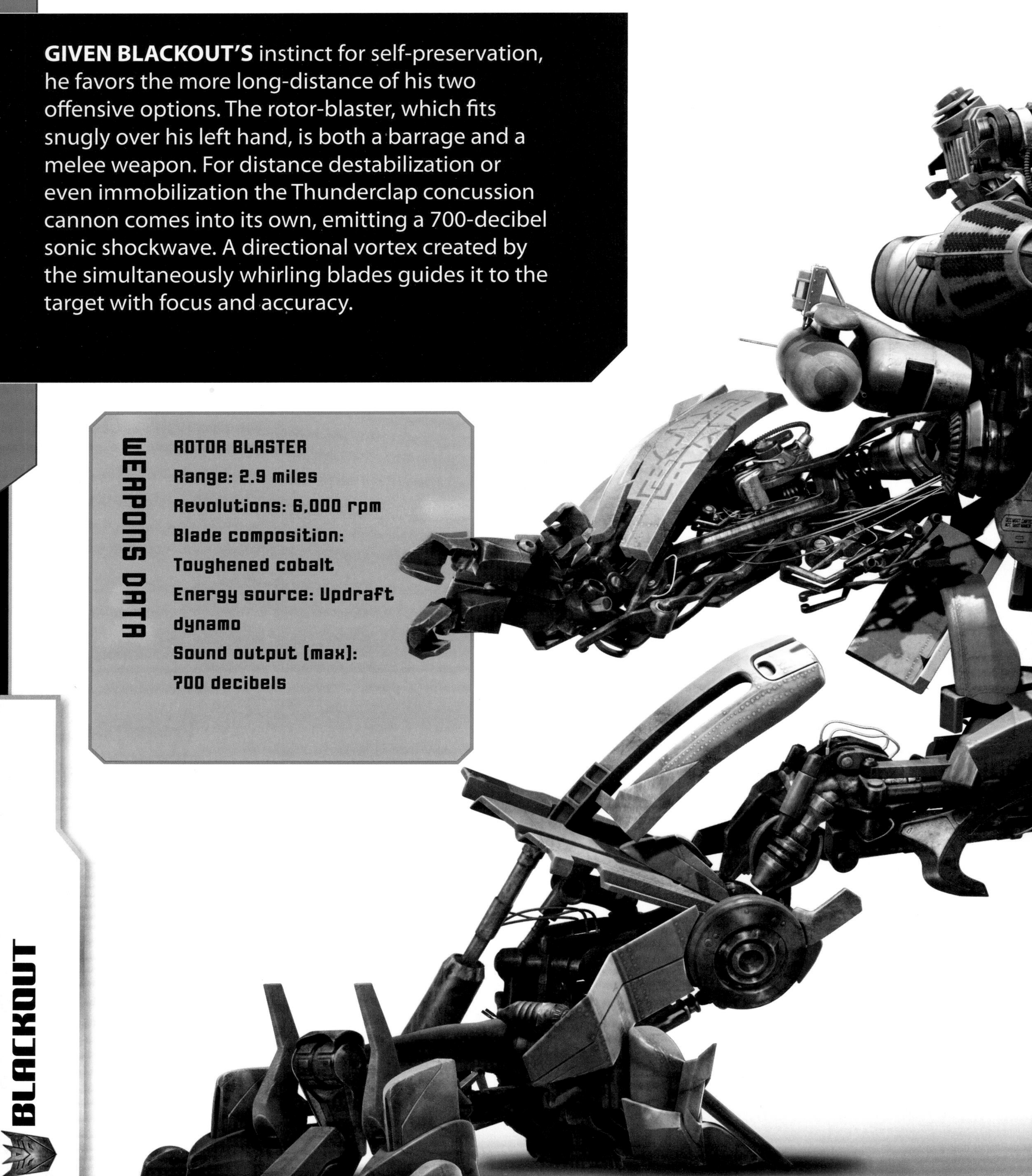

BLACKOUT WEAPON MODE

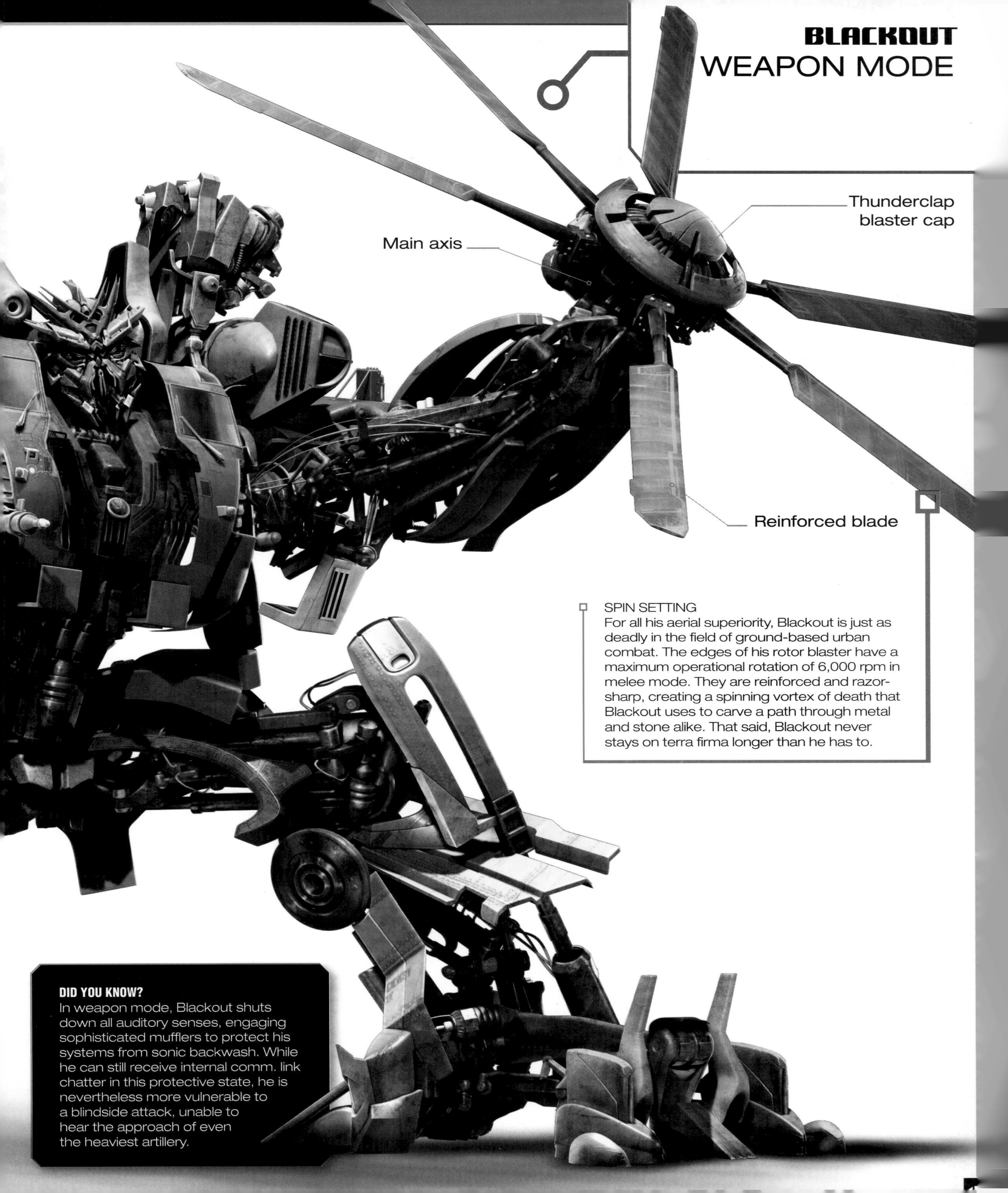

SPIN SETTING

For all his aerial superiority, Blackout is just as deadly in the field of ground-based urban combat. The edges of his rotor blaster have a maximum operational rotation of 6,000 rpm in melee mode. They are reinforced and razor-sharp, creating a spinning vortex of death that Blackout uses to carve a path through metal and stone alike. That said, Blackout never stays on terra firma longer than he has to.

DID YOU KNOW?

In weapon mode, Blackout shuts down all auditory senses, engaging sophisticated mufflers to protect his systems from sonic backwash. While he can still receive internal comm. link chatter in this protective state, he is nevertheless more vulnerable to a blindside attack, unable to hear the approach of even the heaviest artillery.

SCORPONOK
DECEPTICON TRACKER

Debris dispersal vents

LITTLE MORE THAN one step up from a drone trooper, Scorponok nevertheless has a wily, patient, and wholly methodical approach to the business of mayhem that leads one to believe he's a lot smarter than he appears. On Cybertron, Scorponok's preferred modus operandi is to integrate himself with the battle wreckage that littered the planet's once pristine surface, shut down all but the most essential life-support systems, and wait for unwary Autobot patrols.

Face guard

Main drill spindle

Drill cogs

Magno-grip digits

DETERMINEDLY DEADLY

With two forward 20 mm cannons, deploying fragmentation rockets, and a 500 kw electro-static tail stinger, Scorponok is every bit as lethal as Decepticons three or four times his size. He's also infinitely patient. In his preferred subterranean environment, Scorponok will burrow for hundreds of miles, or lay in wait for months at a time.

SCORPONOK
ROBOT MODE

Electrostatic emitter

Stinger sensor rod

TECHNICAL DATA

Length: 8' 8''
Weight: 0.6 metric tons
Strength: Power Level 2

Segmented prehensile tail

UP AND AT 'EM
Scorponok ruthlessly sets about hunting down and eradicating the military personnel who escape the attack on the Qatar airbase. Burrowing under the desert sand, he strikes when the unit threatens to call for reinforcements. The fact that most of Major Lennox's men survive speaks volumes for their own resourcefulness.

JAZZ

AUTOBOT INTELLIGENCE OFFICER

WHATEVER YOU NEED, no matter where in the world (or indeed universe) you are, Jazz can get it for you. His innate understanding of environments, alien or otherwise, and his sheer adaptability make him indispensable on any mission. Jazz absorbs information like a sponge, assimilating languages, culture, and geo-political data at breathtaking speed. Endlessly fascinated by new cultures, Jazz wants in on any kind of exploration mission.

DID YOU KNOW?
Jazz is very fast, both in robot and vehicular mode. His armor plating has a special friction retardant surface, allowing him to almost glide through wind currents.

"WHATEVER YOU DO, DO IT WITH STYLE."

FIRST AMONG EQUALS

Amazingly cool under pressure, Jazz can process raw data and output focused info-feeds in a matter of nano-kliks. As the battle for Cybertron raged on, so the need for Jazz's improvisational tactical projections intensified, and he was soon promoted to First Lieutenant, effectively Optimus Prime's right-hand 'bot.

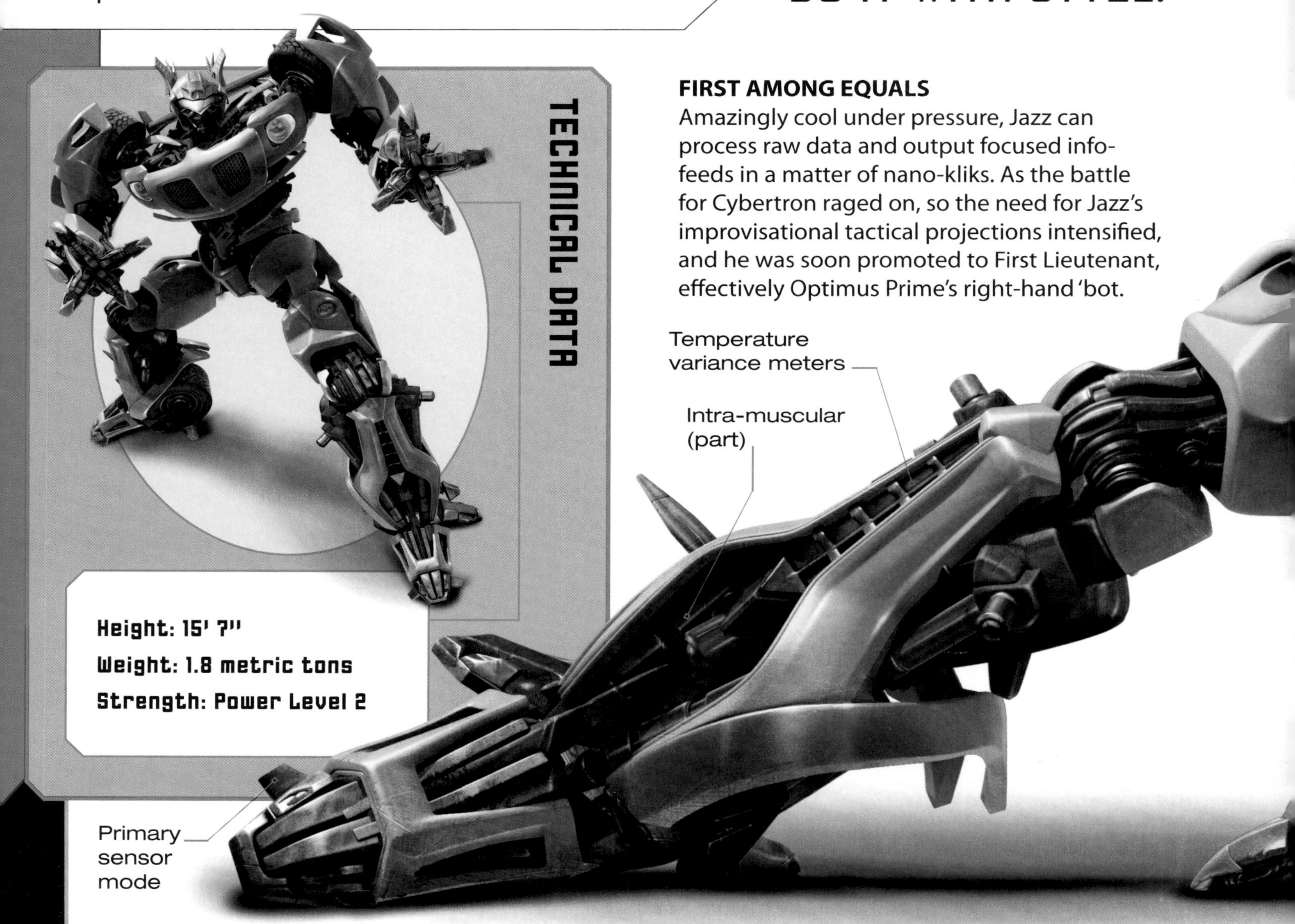

TECHNICAL DATA

Height: 15' 7"
Weight: 1.8 metric tons
Strength: Power Level 2

JAZZ
ROBOT MODE

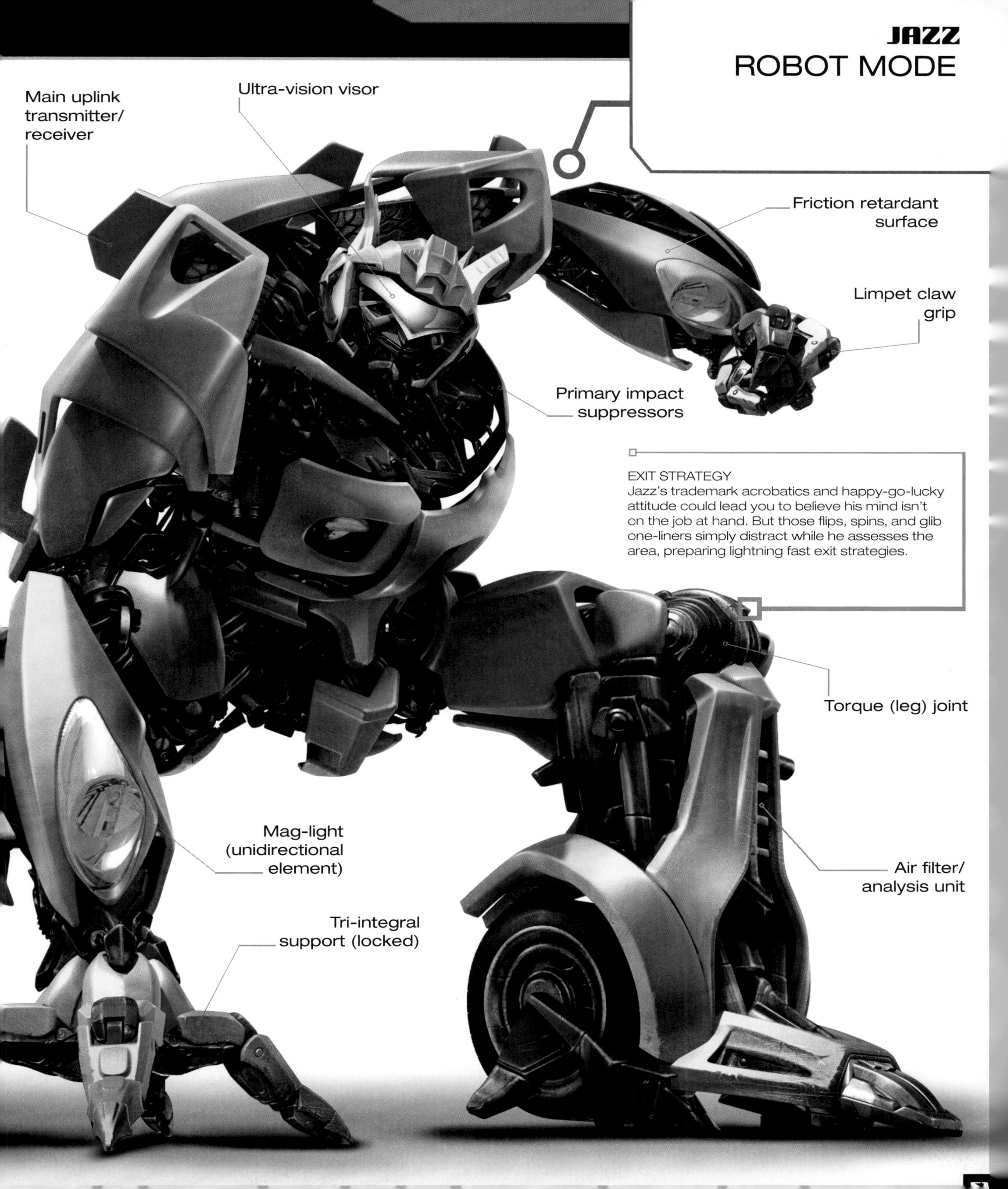

EXIT STRATEGY
Jazz's trademark acrobatics and happy-go-lucky attitude could lead you to believe his mind isn't on the job at hand. But those flips, spins, and glib one-liners simply distract while he assesses the area, preparing lightning fast exit strategies.

JAZZ

IT COMES AS little surprise to anyone that, when selecting a suitable Earth disguise, Jazz opts for something fast, sporty, and utterly eye-catching. The Pontiac Solstice suits him down to the ground as Jazz innately understands the difference between merely functional and plain cool! The other Autobots simply opt for the first vehicle (of comparable size and mass) they clap optics on, whereas Jazz, attuned instantly to all manner of media, sets his sights just a little higher.

DID YOU KNOW?
Jazz is always first to put the pedal to the metal, utilizing his unique "speed of thought" acceleration feature, which cuts out several internal gear processes.

VEHICLE MODE

KEEPING UP APPEARANCES

If Jazz has a character flaw, it's that he's unwilling to engage in combat in vehicular mode. He hates the idea of picking up a dent or scratch to his bodywork, and would rather transform to robot mode and go for hand-to-hand combat, or take up a position outside the main combat zone and call the shots.

Friction retardant surface

Main antenna/ receptor

Recessed traction studs

TECHNICAL DATA

Top speed: 400 mph

0–60 in: 1.07 seconds

Engine: 450 HP

Max haulage: 30 metric tons

DID YOU KNOW?

Jazz can simultaneously receive visual and audio feed from six hundred dedicated wavelengths and channels, instantly decoding or unscrambling top-secret communiqués.

NATURAL SELECTION

Arriving on Earth, Jazz makes sure that he lands in a neighborhood in which the car showrooms reflect a certain spending power. Call it vanity or call it evolutionary natural selection, Jazz knows what he will or won't be seen dead in.

DID YOU KNOW?
In weapon mode, Jazz likes to charge at the enemy using his extendable wheels like roller skates. This lightning fast attack, combined with his battle shield, has broken sieges that have frustrated battalions of Autobots. Jazz can also generate a low level forcefield to protect his Spark chamber, but he sometimes redirects this to safeguard his bodywork.

WEAPONS DATA

CRYO-EMITTER

Range: 0.9 miles

Minimum temperature: -400 degrees-c

Shield composition: Tri-tanium

Energy source: Freon core

Guidance unit: Laser

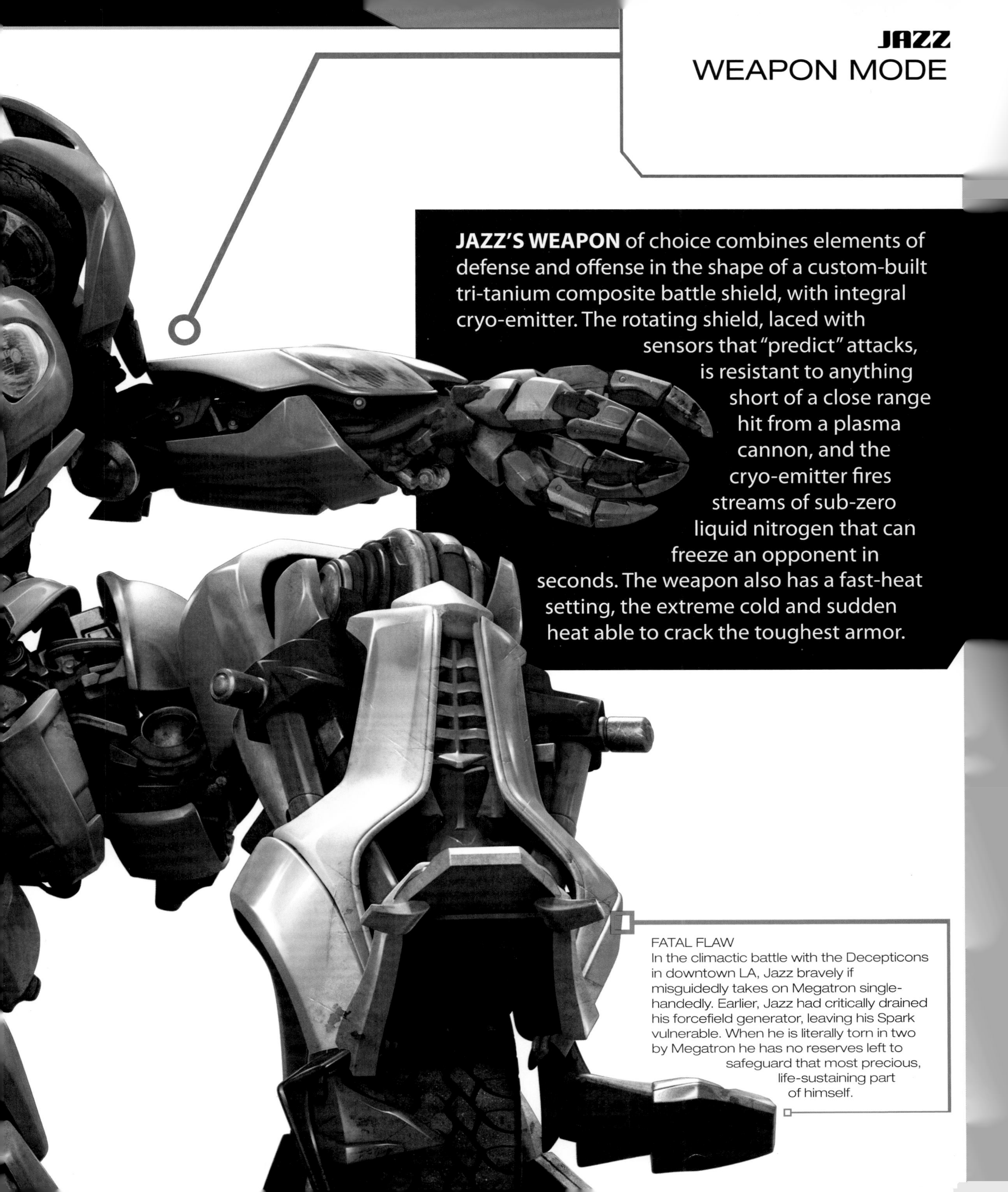

JAZZ
WEAPON MODE

JAZZ'S WEAPON of choice combines elements of defense and offense in the shape of a custom-built tri-tanium composite battle shield, with integral cryo-emitter. The rotating shield, laced with sensors that "predict" attacks, is resistant to anything short of a close range hit from a plasma cannon, and the cryo-emitter fires streams of sub-zero liquid nitrogen that can freeze an opponent in seconds. The weapon also has a fast-heat setting, the extreme cold and sudden heat able to crack the toughest armor.

FATAL FLAW
In the climactic battle with the Decepticons in downtown LA, Jazz bravely if misguidedly takes on Megatron single-handedly. Earlier, Jazz had critically drained his forcefield generator, leaving his Spark vulnerable. When he is literally torn in two by Megatron he has no reserves left to safeguard that most precious, life-sustaining part of himself.

RATCHET
AUTOBOT MEDIC

THOUGH HIS OFFICIAL TITLE is Medical Officer, Ratchet is more of an all-round, one-'bot emergency search and rescue specialist. Saving lives is what he does, but actually getting to those in need of treatment is his real forte. Often those who want his help are in hostile or inaccessible environments, and the tougher the terrain, the more Ratchet likes it! There's nowhere he won't go, no place he fears to tread, and no obstacle he can't overcome.

DID YOU KNOW?
Ratchet is built for strength rather than speed. His durable, heavy-duty armature ensures he gets where he's going in one piece... but not necessarily at the double.

"KILL OR CURE, FOR ME IT'S AN OPTION."

TECHNICAL DATA

Height: 20' 1"
Weight: 3.4 metric tons
Strength: Power Level 4

ALL DUE RESPECT
Ratchet is just as much at home in the realms of diplomacy and negotiation as he is on the battlefield. Before the Great War, Optimus Prime appointed Ratchet his chief liaison to the High Council of Ancients. With great tact, Ratchet was able to heal many a division between state and senate.

FIRST IMPRESSIONS
Ratchet's finely attuned medical sensors are always running and he is aware of even microscopic physiological changes in those around him. When Ratchet first encounters Sam and Mikaela, he notes raised pheromone levels in Sam, concluding that the boy is ready to mate.

Storage for cutting tools

ROBOT MODE

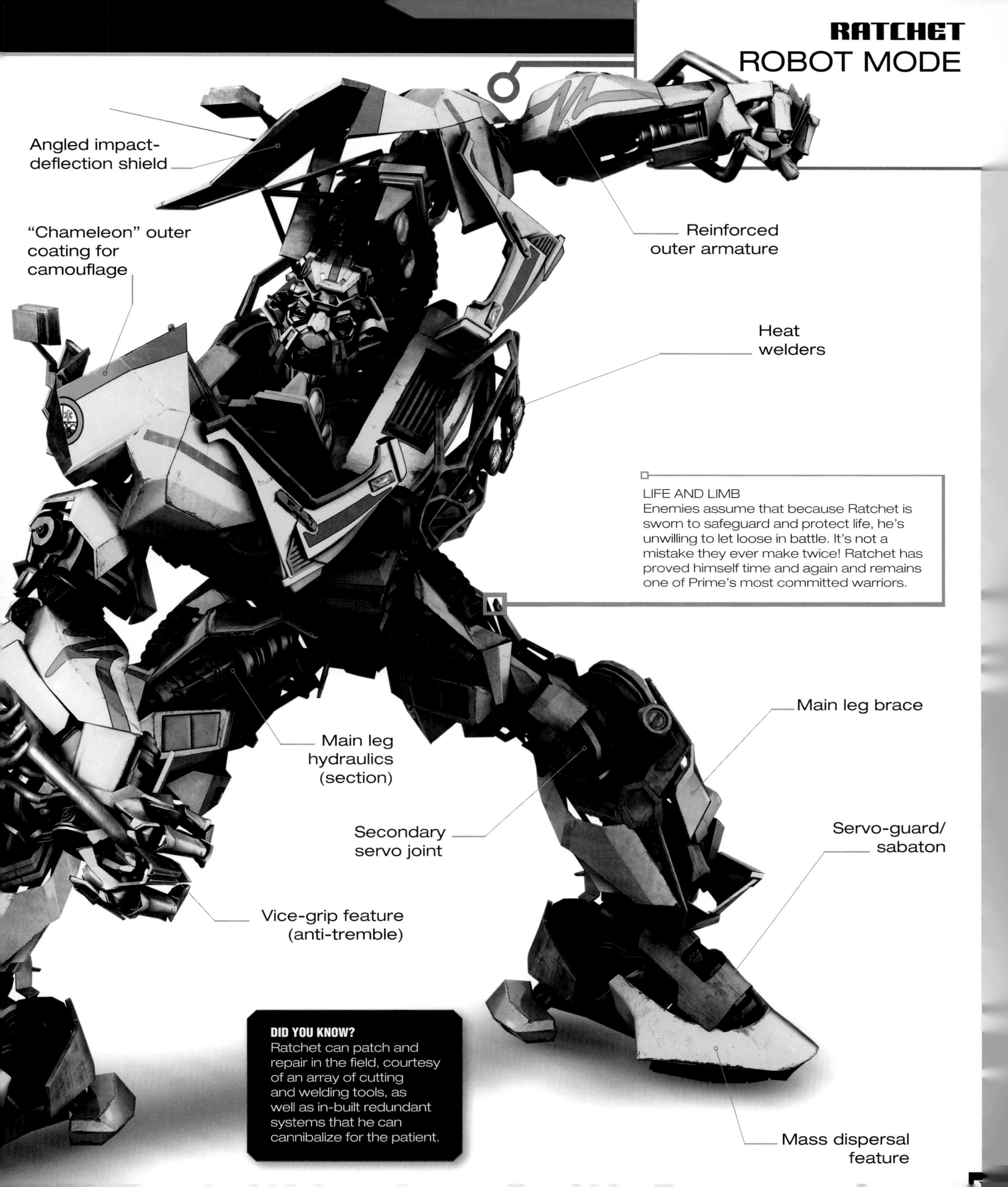

LIFE AND LIMB
Enemies assume that because Ratchet is sworn to safeguard and protect life, he's unwilling to let loose in battle. It's not a mistake they ever make twice! Ratchet has proved himself time and again and remains one of Prime's most committed warriors.

DID YOU KNOW?
Ratchet can patch and repair in the field, courtesy of an array of cutting and welding tools, as well as in-built redundant systems that he can cannibalize for the patient.

RATCHET

RATCHET'S DRAMATIC ARRIVAL on Earth brings ambulances and fire trucks screaming to the scene, just as Ratchet had planned. Having chosen his downtown landing site and avoided any loss of life, all Ratchet has to do is wait. The occupants of the first Hummer H2 rescue vehicle on the scene are oblivious to the alien rays that map and detail every inch of their vehicle. Moments later, from the site of the crashlanding, an identical Hummer H2 emerges.

DID YOU KNOW?
Ratchet's forward ramming bars are fashioned from a molded silicate/metal amalgam of incredible density.

Load-locking gantry

Charging indicators

Rear load bearing ramp

All-terrain tires

Force distribution system

THE ONE

Long ago Ratchet told himself, "You can't save them all." It's a truism that his logic center accepts but his Spark routinely overrules. He could save a hundred lives but it's the one he can't save that haunts him. When that individual is not just an ally but a close friend too, being unable to save them hurts a thousand times more.

BIG NOISE

He's got a siren and he knows how to use it! When it comes to getting the Allspark to Mission City in the fastest time possible, Ratchet proves invaluable. Piercing blasts of modulated sound clear a path through the heavy traffic so the convoy of Autobots and military vehicles can pass.

DID YOU KNOW?
Ratchet can haul or push four times his own weight and mass, using a vibrational force distribution system located under his main chassis.

RATCHET
VEHICLE MODE

TECHNICAL DATA

Top speed: 230 mph

0–60 in: 3.65 seconds

Engine: 650 HP

Max haulage: 134 metric tons

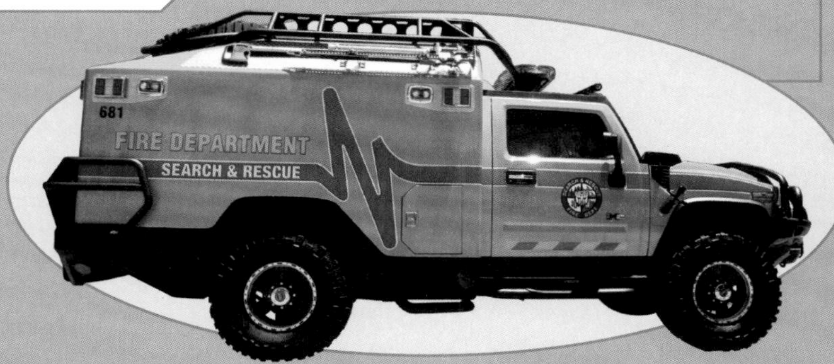
681
FIRE DEPARTMENT
SEARCH & RESCUE

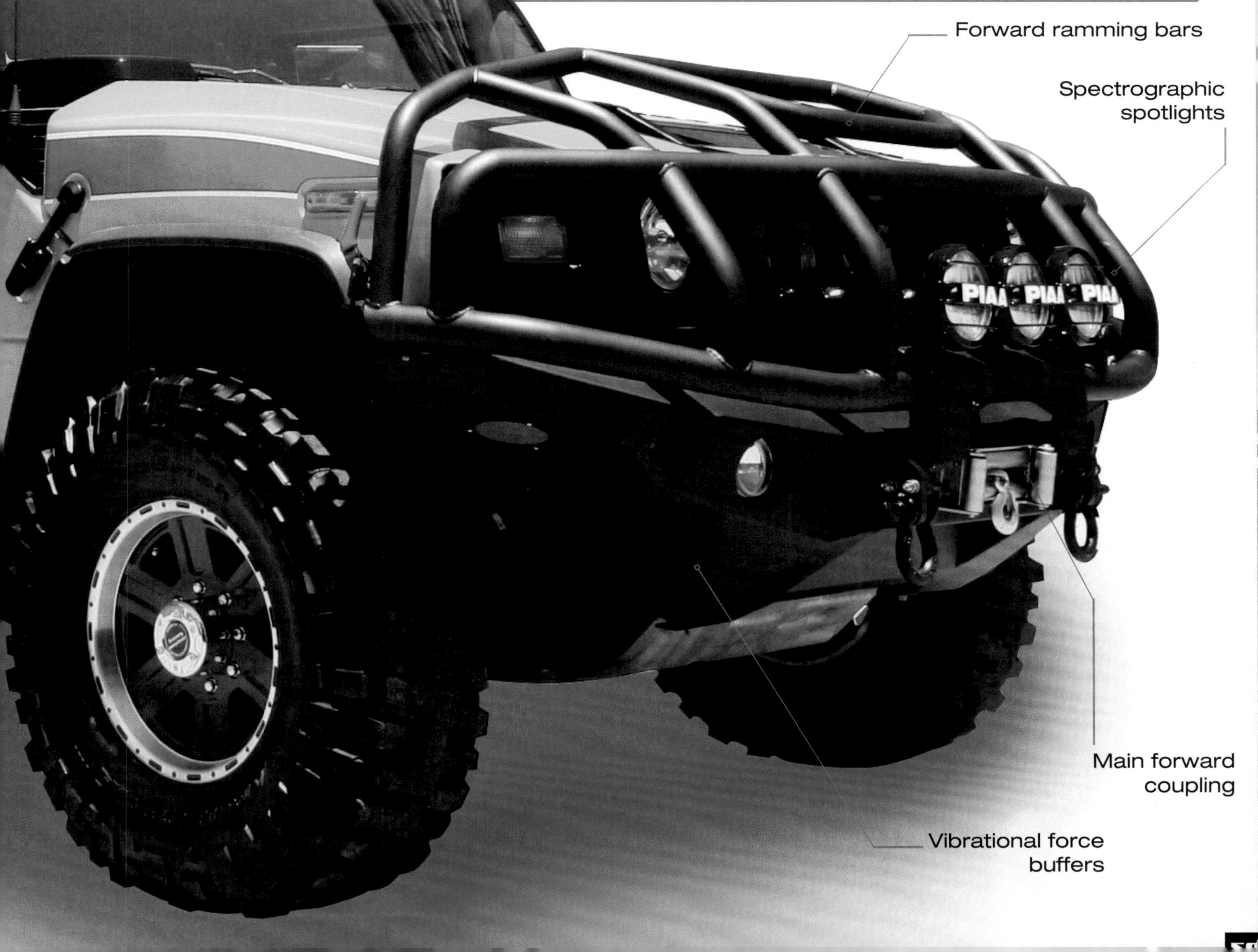
"Daylight" halogen lamps (x4)
Emergency signals
Forward ramming bars
Spectrographic spotlights
PIAA PIAA PIAA
Main forward coupling
Vibrational force buffers

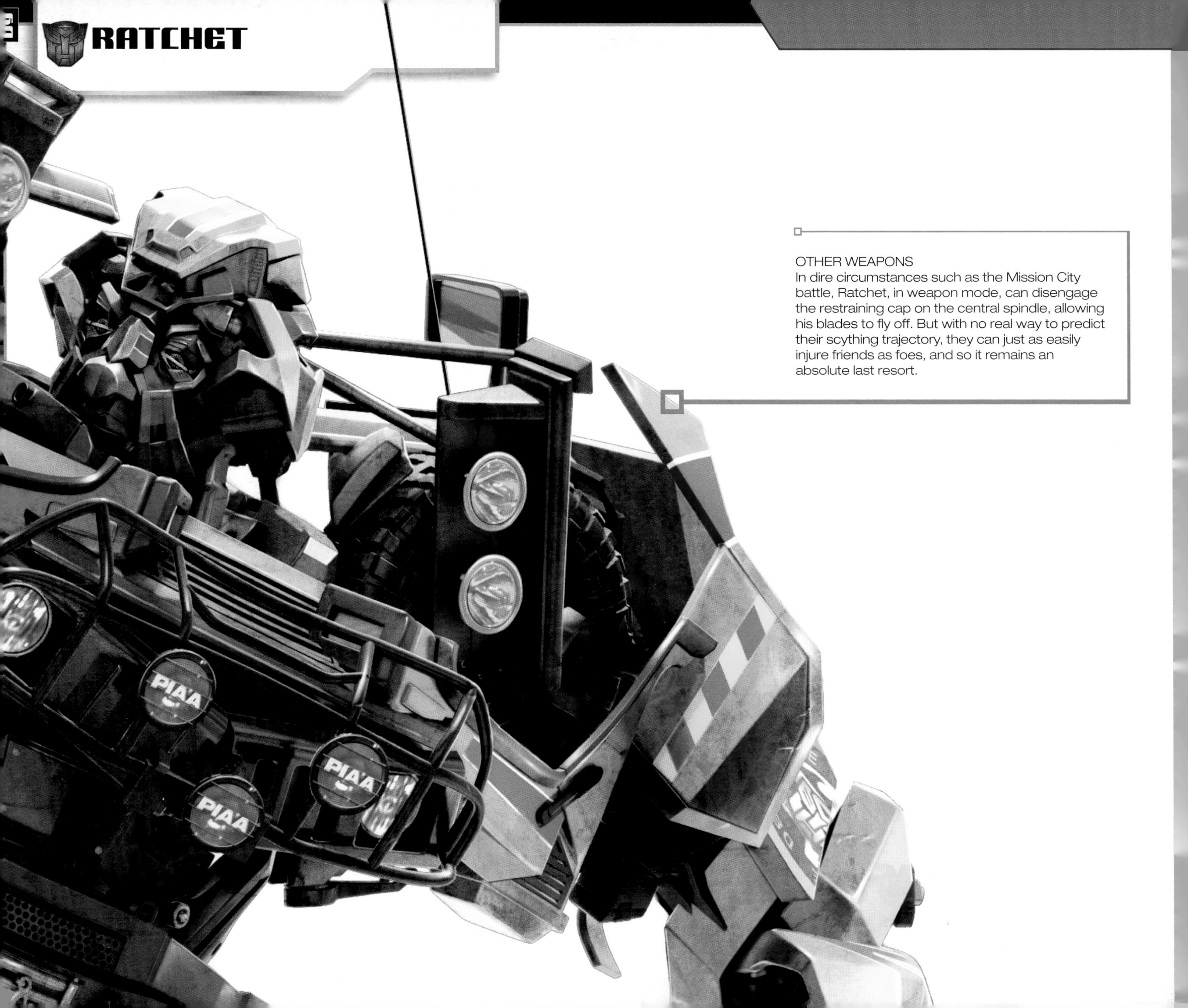

OTHER WEAPONS
In dire circumstances such as the Mission City battle, Ratchet, in weapon mode, can disengage the restraining cap on the central spindle, allowing his blades to fly off. But with no real way to predict their scything trajectory, they can just as easily injure friends as foes, and so it remains an absolute last resort.

RATCHET
WEAPON MODE

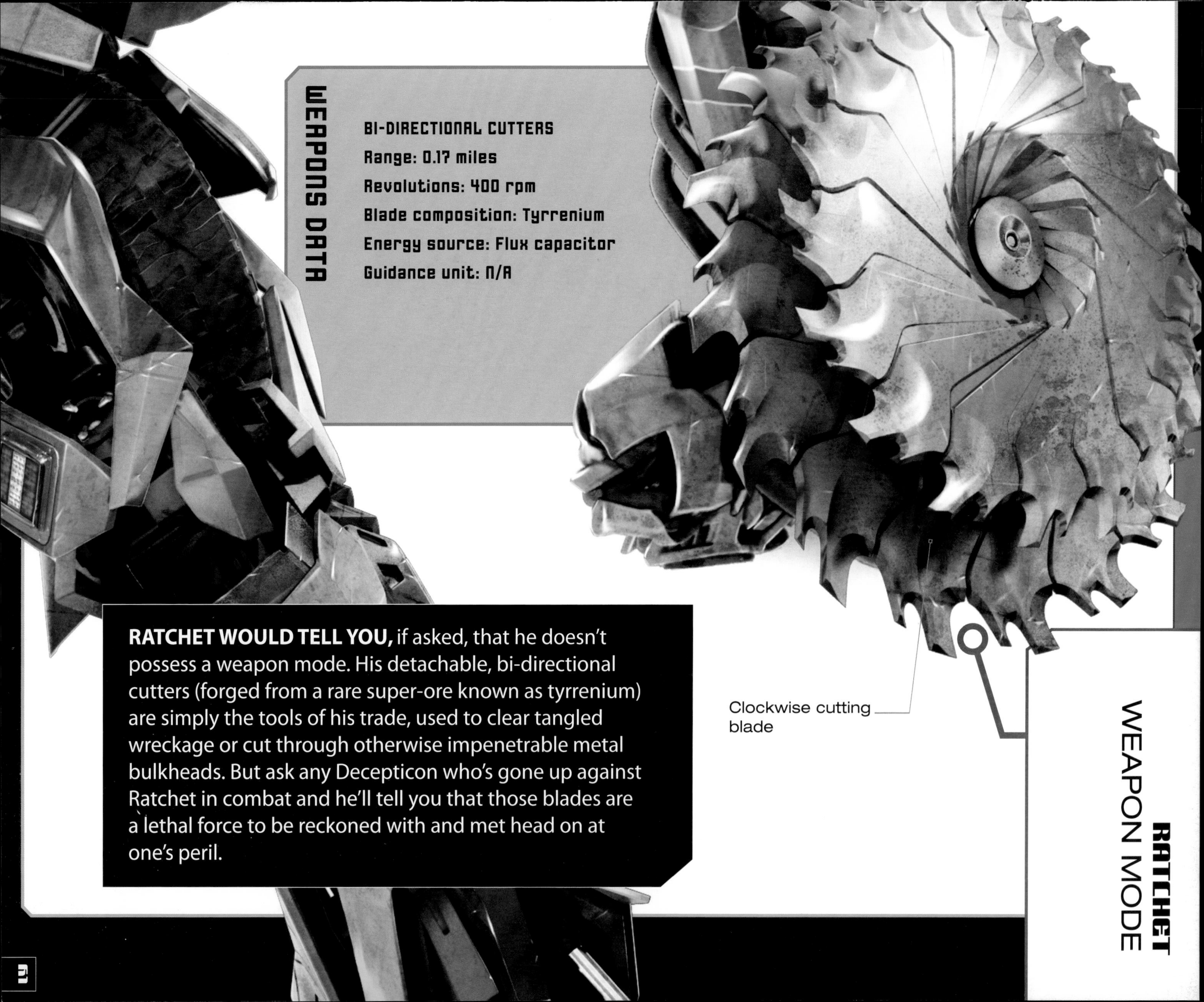

WEAPONS DATA

BI-DIRECTIONAL CUTTERS

Range: 0.17 miles

Revolutions: 400 rpm

Blade composition: Tyrrenium

Energy source: Flux capacitor

Guidance unit: N/A

RATCHET WOULD TELL YOU, if asked, that he doesn't possess a weapon mode. His detachable, bi-directional cutters (forged from a rare super-ore known as tyrrenium) are simply the tools of his trade, used to clear tangled wreckage or cut through otherwise impenetrable metal bulkheads. But ask any Decepticon who's gone up against Ratchet in combat and he'll tell you that those blades are a lethal force to be reckoned with and met head on at one's peril.

IRONHIDE

AUTOBOT MASTER-AT-ARMS

WHILE MANY AUTOBOTS had to adapt to the role of warrior, Ironhide was in the thick of things long before Megatron declared war—a veteran of countless brawls, with the battle scars to prove it. Ironhide may come across as taciturn and cantankerous, often grunting and snorting instead of vocalising, but he'd lay down his life in an instant if it meant others made it out alive. Thing is, he's just too stubborn and too tough to bite the big one!

"I DON'T GO AROUND... I GO THROUGH!"

DID YOU KNOW?
Although Ironhide wields a plethora of long-range weapons, he prefers to get up close and personal with the enemy forces. His battle-strategy often amounts to "charge!"

TECHNICAL DATA

Height: 25'
Weight: 4.8 metric tonnes
Strength: Power Level 3

UN-CIVIL DEFENSE
Although Cybertron knew peace for long periods of its pre-civil war history, that didn't mean its inhabitants were defenseless. Ironhide was the field commander of Cybertron's civil defense militia, a tireless crack unit that saw off numerous threats from other worlds.

IRONHIDE
ROBOT MODE

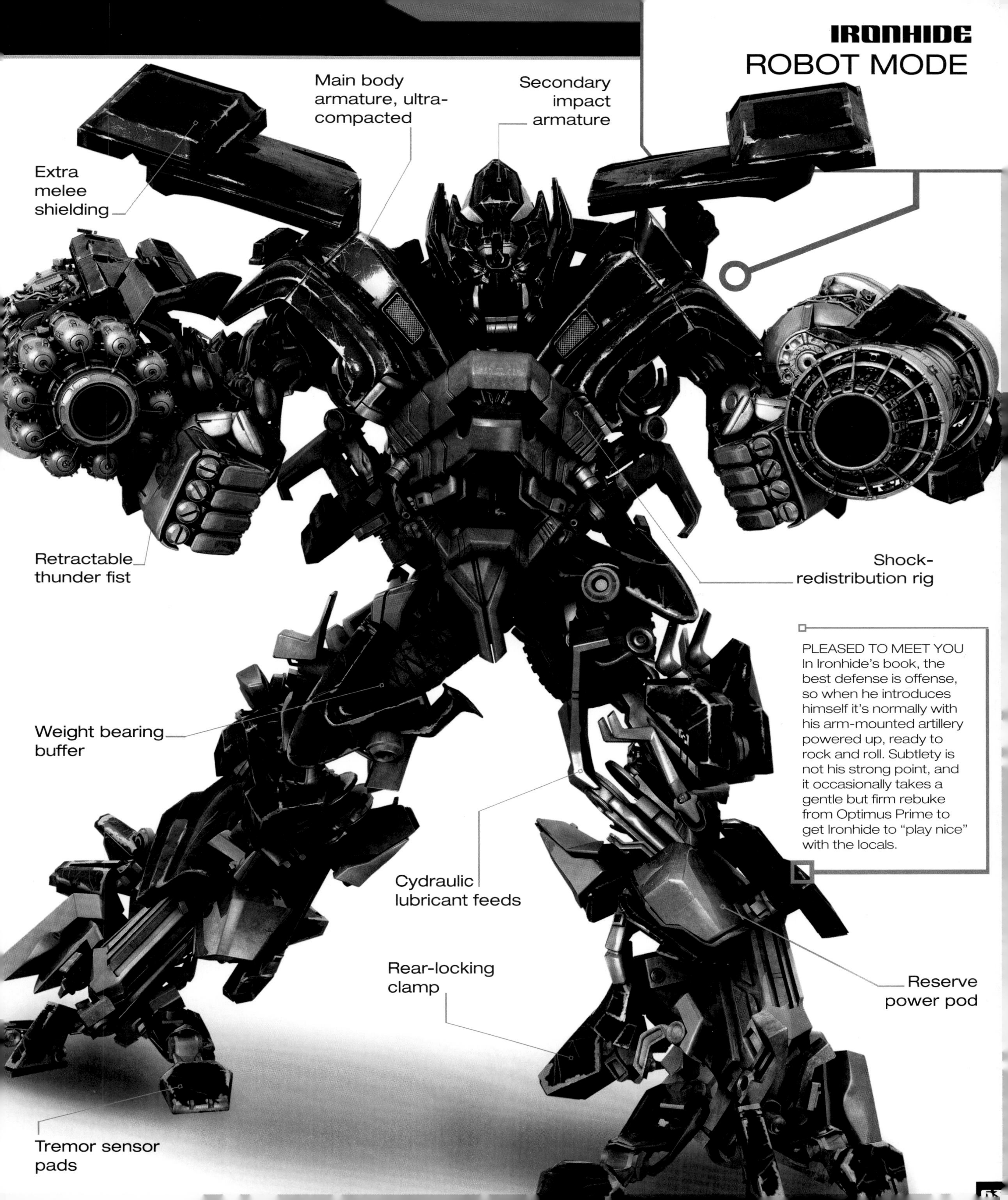

PLEASED TO MEET YOU
In Ironhide's book, the best defense is offense, so when he introduces himself it's normally with his arm-mounted artillery powered up, ready to rock and roll. Subtlety is not his strong point, and it occasionally takes a gentle but firm rebuke from Optimus Prime to get Ironhide to "play nice" with the locals.

IRONHIDE

FIRST IMPRESSIONS COUNT, and Ironhide likes to make a statement of intent that leaves no room for misinterpretation. Though modeled on a GMC TopKick pickup truck, Ironhide's vehicular mode looks and feels like a tank, especially if you're in a head-on collision with it. Big, bold, and utterly all-terrain, Ironhide's vehicle form has virtually relentless forward momentum and heavy-duty armor plating to back it up.

DID YOU KNOW?
Ironhide's robot mode weapons are stored under his vehicle mode's chassis, below the driver and passenger doors. They can be rolled out and fired even at high speed.

HARD TARGET
Although resistant to damage and something of an unstoppable force, Ironhide is not indestructible. Therefore, to frustrate and confuse the enemy, Ironhide's vehicular mode comes with a built-in strobe lighting effect, which makes it hard for opponents to get a solid target lock.

IRONHIDE
VEHICLE MODE

TECHNICAL DATA

Top speed: 110 mph

0–60 in: 0.8 seconds

Engine: 350 HP

Max haulage: 200 metric tons

GROUND ASSAULT
While willing and able to go it alone, Ironhide never forgets he's part of a team. His mud-grappler tires, load-bearing bed, and high-jacked suspension enable him to shift three times his own weight. His multi-function rear section can also carry fuel and supplies.

WEAPONS DATA

RADIAL MISSILE LAUNCHER

Range: 1.5 miles

Max yield: 10 kt

Warhead: Plasma

Firing rate: 3 rounds per second

DID YOU KNOW?
Over the years, Ironhide has been dubbed Optimus Prime's "big stick," a reference to his sheer, drop-of-a-hat willingness to use whatever weapons he has available to maximum, devastating effect. Where Prime exercises restraint above all else, Ironhide simply exercises his trigger finger!

WEAPON MOD

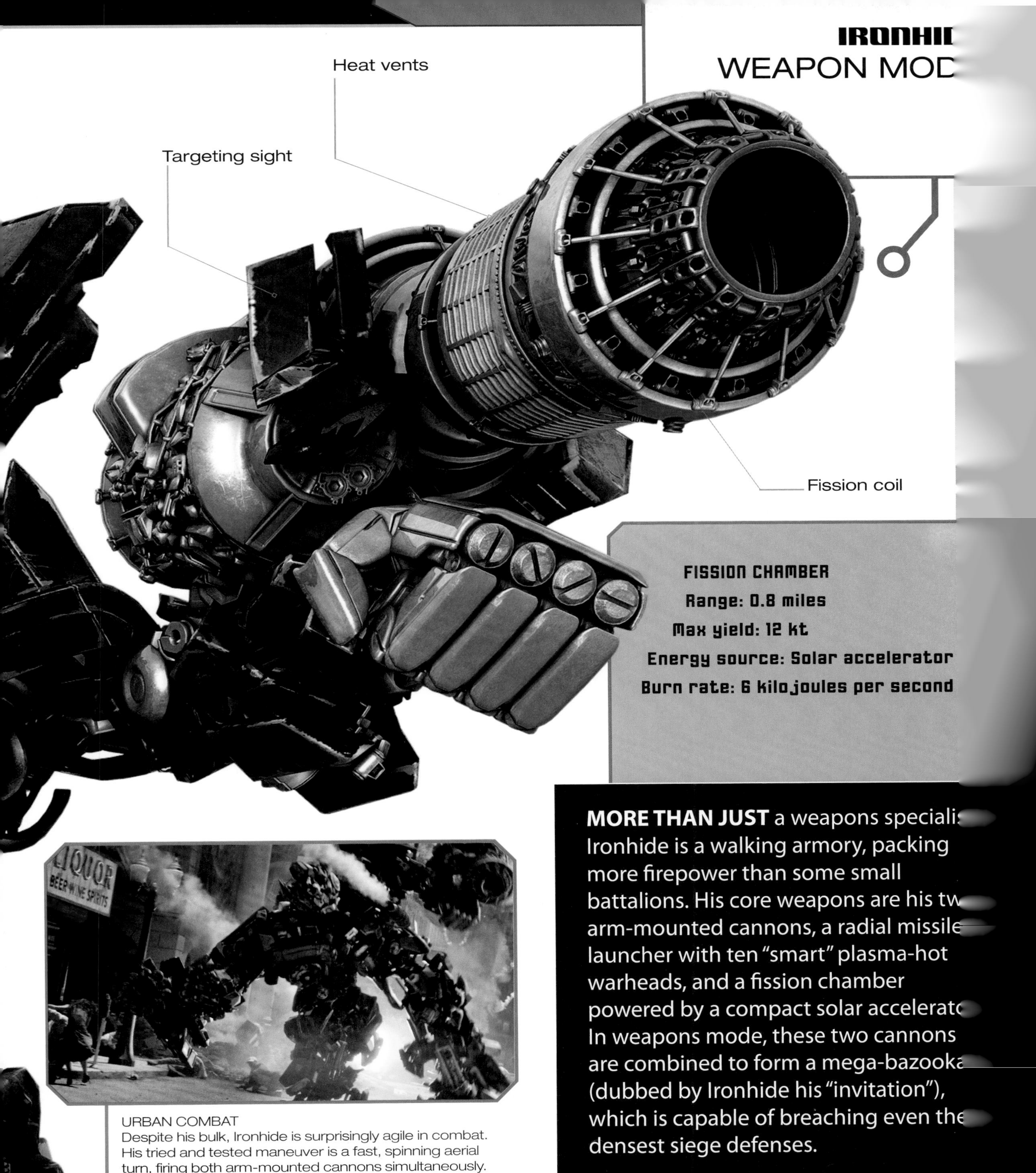

FISSION CHAMBER

Range: 0.8 miles

Max yield: 12 kt

Energy source: Solar accelerator

Burn rate: 6 kilojoules per second

MORE THAN JUST a weapons speciali Ironhide is a walking armory, packing more firepower than some small battalions. His core weapons are his tw arm-mounted cannons, a radial missile launcher with ten "smart" plasma-hot warheads, and a fission chamber powered by a compact solar accelerat In weapons mode, these two cannons are combined to form a mega-bazook (dubbed by Ironhide his "invitation"), which is capable of breaching even the densest siege defenses.

URBAN COMBAT
Despite his bulk, Ironhide is surprisingly agile in combat. His tried and tested maneuver is a fast, spinning aerial turn, firing both arm-mounted cannons simultaneously. A specialist in urban combat, Ironhide uses tight spaces to his advantage, leaving a foe little option for retreat.

STARSCREAM

DECEPTICON AIR COMMANDER

UTTERLY SELF-SERVING, shock-trooper Starscream neither cares for nor believes in anything save his own personal advancement and gratification. While he appears to do Megatron's bidding, in truth he's biding his time, awaiting the perfect opportunity to seize power. Starscream knows that a direct challenge is out of the question, but should a power vacuum appear, he will be ready. In the meantime, he just focuses on amassing the sort of headcount that will get him noticed.

DID YOU KNOW?
In his F-22 (Lockheed Raptor) aerial mode, Starscream carries four laser-guided missiles with thermo-reactive warheads that burn at over 1,000 degrees centigrade. He also access these missiles in robot mode.

"I HAVE THREE PRIORITIES... ME, MYSELF, AND I."

HEIR APPARENT
When Megatron's life-functions are apparently terminated in Mission City, Starscream is waiting in the wings. After the battle, he declares himself "interim" commander-in-chief of the Decepticon army. Whether he can hang onto power remains to be seen!

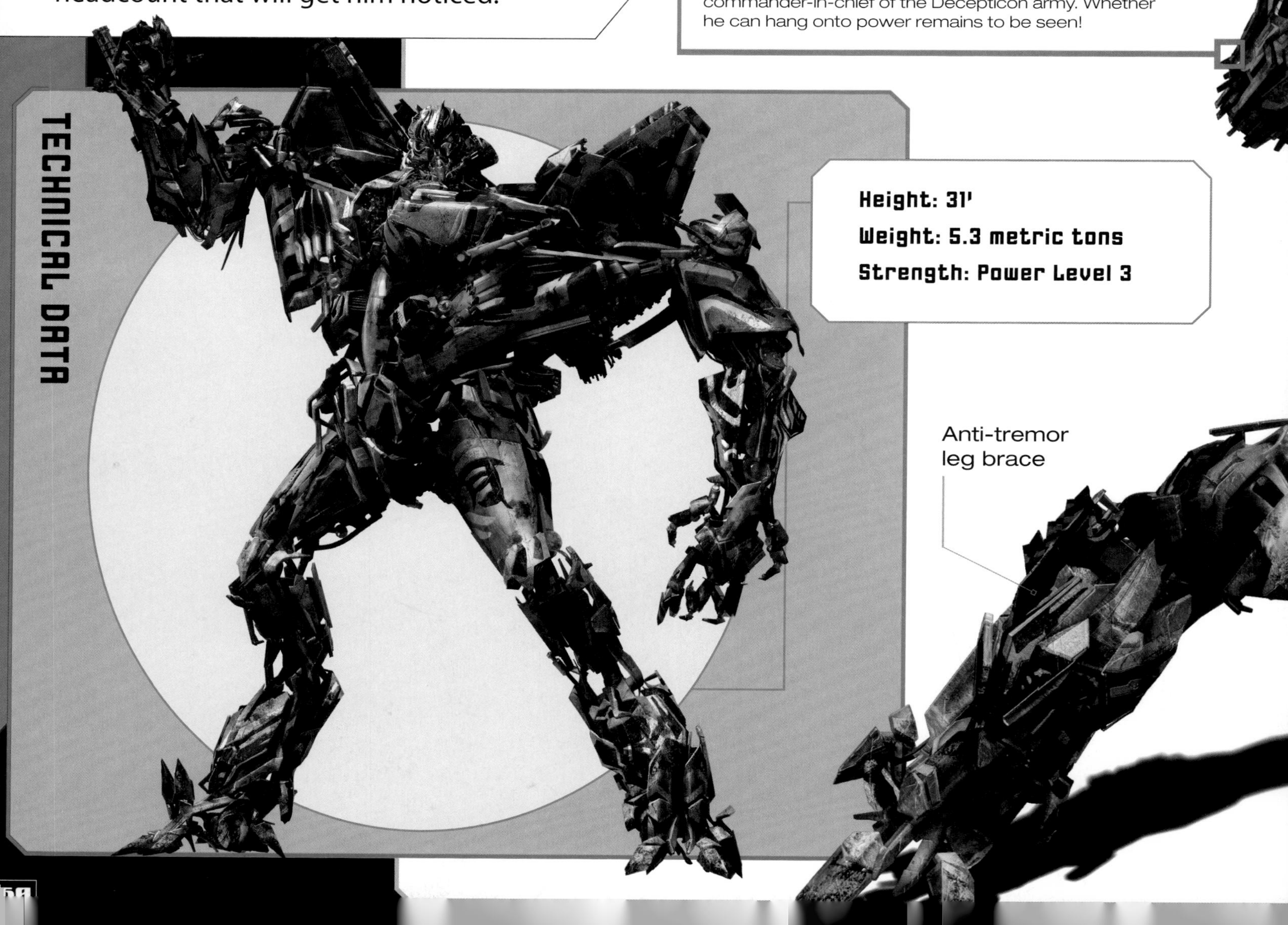

TECHNICAL DATA

Height: 31'
Weight: 5.3 metric tons
Strength: Power Level 3

STARSCREAM
ROBOT MODE

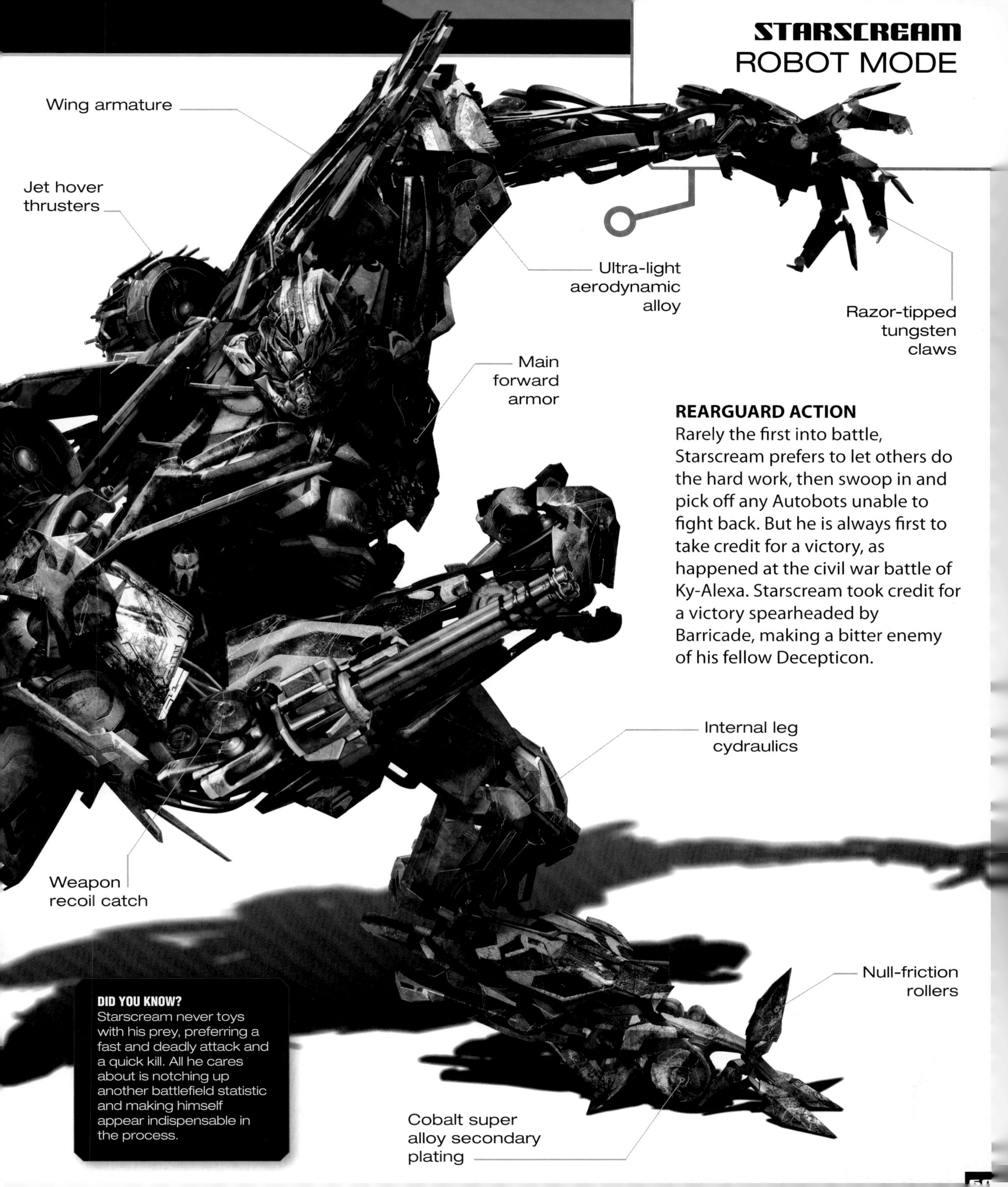

REARGUARD ACTION

Rarely the first into battle, Starscream prefers to let others do the hard work, then swoop in and pick off any Autobots unable to fight back. But he is always first to take credit for a victory, as happened at the civil war battle of Ky-Alexa. Starscream took credit for a victory spearheaded by Barricade, making a bitter enemy of his fellow Decepticon.

DID YOU KNOW?

Starscream never toys with his prey, preferring a fast and deadly attack and a quick kill. All he cares about is notching up another battlefield statistic and making himself appear indispensable in the process.

WEAPONS DATA

HUNTER MISSILE LAUNCHER
Range: 1.3 miles
Strength: Power Level 5
Burn yield: 1,000 degrees-c
Warhead: White phosphorus
Firing rate: Every 2 seconds or 6 in cluster

ARTILLERY CANNON
Range: 0.4 miles
Energy source: Half-life dynamo
Firing rate: 140 rounds per second

DID YOU KNOW?
Starscream's hunter missiles come with a thermo-reactive warhead that burns at over 1,000 degrees centigrade on impact, consuming targets utterly.

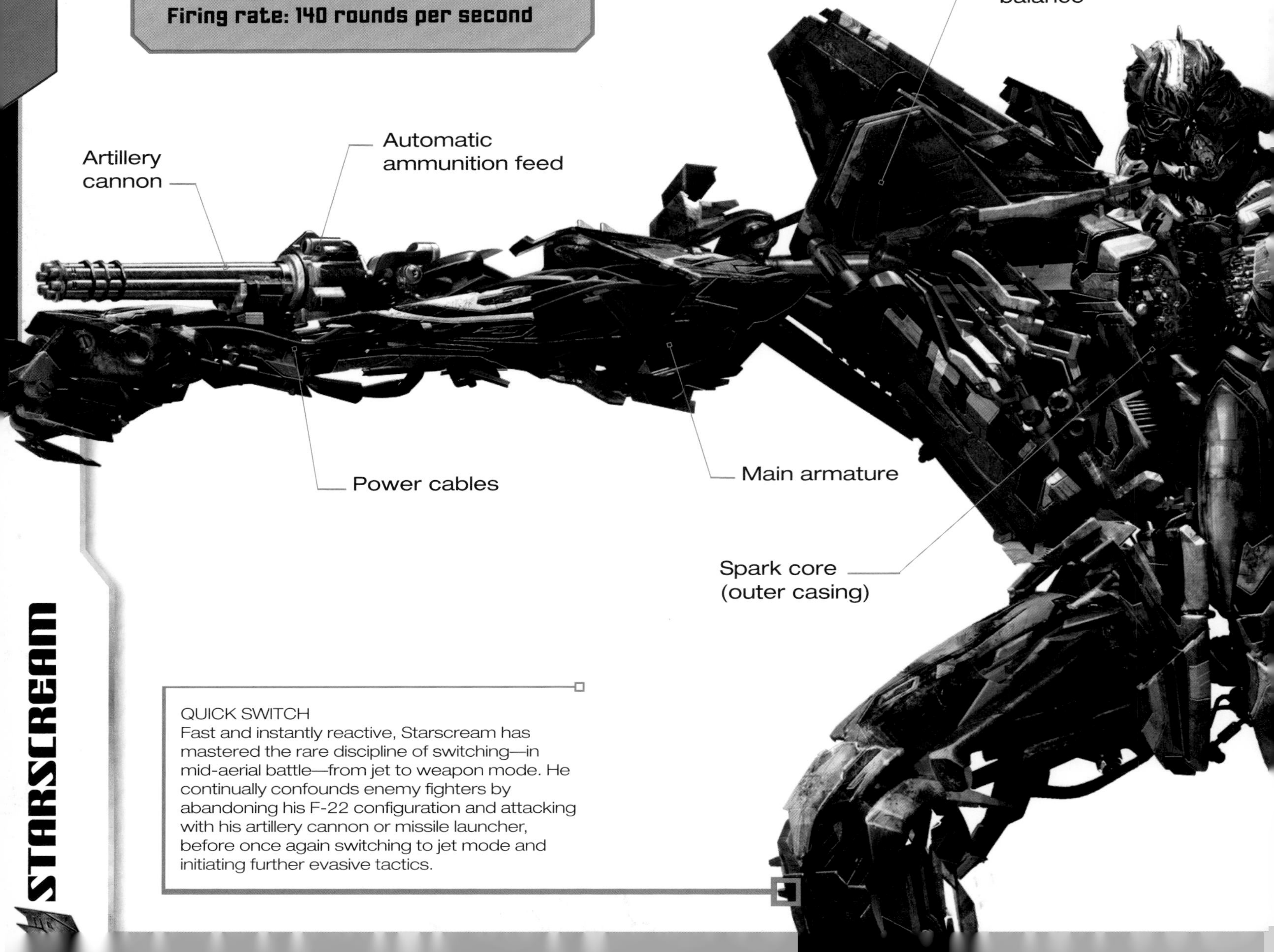

QUICK SWITCH
Fast and instantly reactive, Starscream has mastered the rare discipline of switching—in mid-aerial battle—from jet to weapon mode. He continually confounds enemy fighters by abandoning his F-22 configuration and attacking with his artillery cannon or missile launcher, before once again switching to jet mode and initiating further evasive tactics.

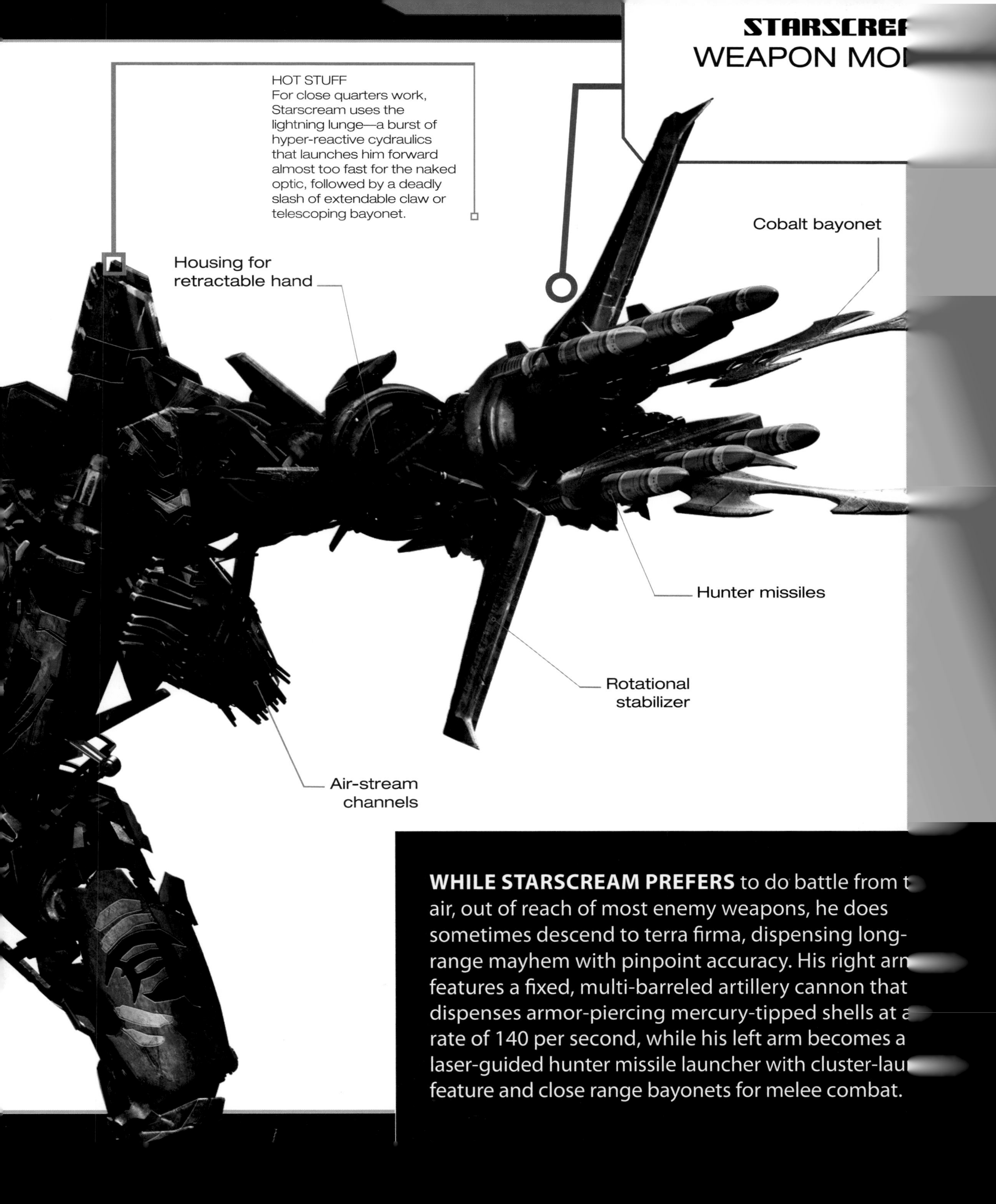

HOT STUFF
For close quarters work, Starscream uses the lightning lunge—a burst of hyper-reactive cydraulics that launches him forward almost too fast for the naked optic, followed by a deadly slash of extendable claw or telescoping bayonet.

WHILE STARSCREAM PREFERS to do battle from t air, out of reach of most enemy weapons, he does sometimes descend to terra firma, dispensing long-range mayhem with pinpoint accuracy. His right arn features a fixed, multi-barreled artillery cannon that dispenses armor-piercing mercury-tipped shells at a rate of 140 per second, while his left arm becomes a laser-guided hunter missile launcher with cluster-lau feature and close range bayonets for melee combat.

SIDESWIPE
AUTOBOT WARRIOR

WHILE AUTOBOTS AREN'T really supposed to relish war, it's fair to say that Sideswipe was built to fight. Part of a latter generation of Autobots forged in a time of war, Sideswipe was thrust directly into the fray, his battlefield instincts fully formed, and every single gear and cog attuned to the cut and thrust of combat. In Sideswipe's defence, fighting is all he's ever known, but still his actions and tactics are not so much direct as merciless.

DID YOU KNOW?
Sideswipe's robot form is all about aerodynamic, quicksilver motion. Two of his vehicle mode wheels act as hyper-velocity skates, allowing him to close the distance between himself and an enemy in a fraction of a second.

Rotational arch

Secondary/ reserve blade

TECHNICAL DATA

Height: 25' 2'
Weight: 2.9 metric tons
Strength: Power Level 3

HEADS WILL ROLL
Whatever the job, however brutal or dirty it gets, Sideswipe is unflinching in what he sees with simple clarity as his duty. He'll see the mission through, however many heads have got to roll. War is mean and messy, and Sideswipe is unapologetic about reflecting that in his ways and methods.

"IT'S A DIRTY JOB, BUT SOMEONE'S GOT TO DO IT."

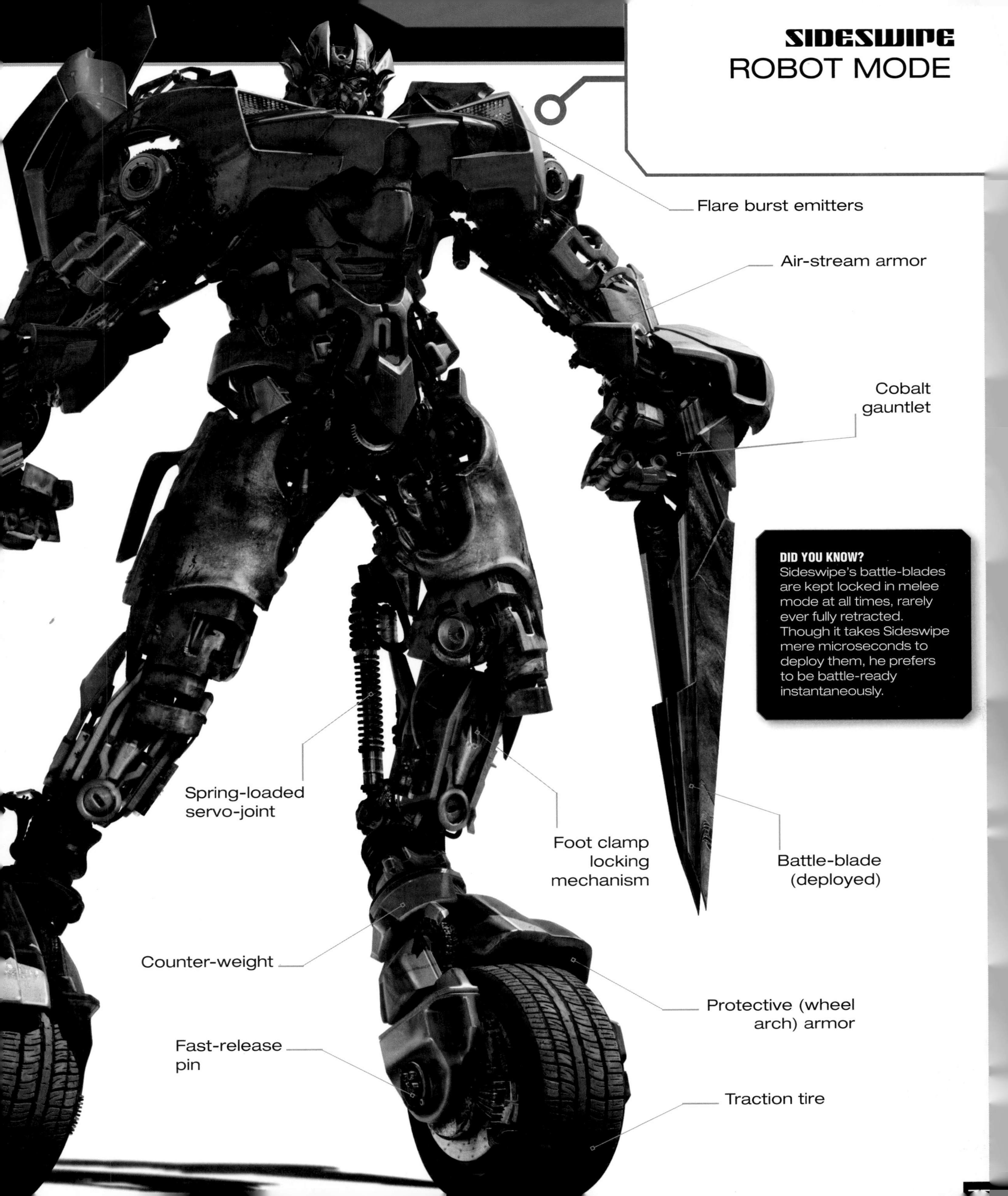
SIDESWIPE
ROBOT MODE
Flare burst emitters
Air-stream armor
Cobalt gauntlet
DID YOU KNOW?
Sideswipe's battle-blades are kept locked in melee mode at all times, rarely ever fully retracted. Though it takes Sideswipe mere microseconds to deploy them, he prefers to be battle-ready instantaneously.
Spring-loaded servo-joint
Foot clamp locking mechanism
Battle-blade (deployed)
Counter-weight
Protective (wheel arch) armor
Fast-release pin
Traction tire

SIDESWIPE

IF ASKED, SIDESWIPE would tell you he doesn't care what he looks like—all he cares about is speed. If that means sleek, low-slung styling, and smooth, impeccably molded bodywork then so be it. But some suspect that Sideswipe is vainer than he lets on, and wouldn't have anything but the latest concept model. His earth form, modeled on a new range Corvette, is fast, powerful, and direct—much like him!

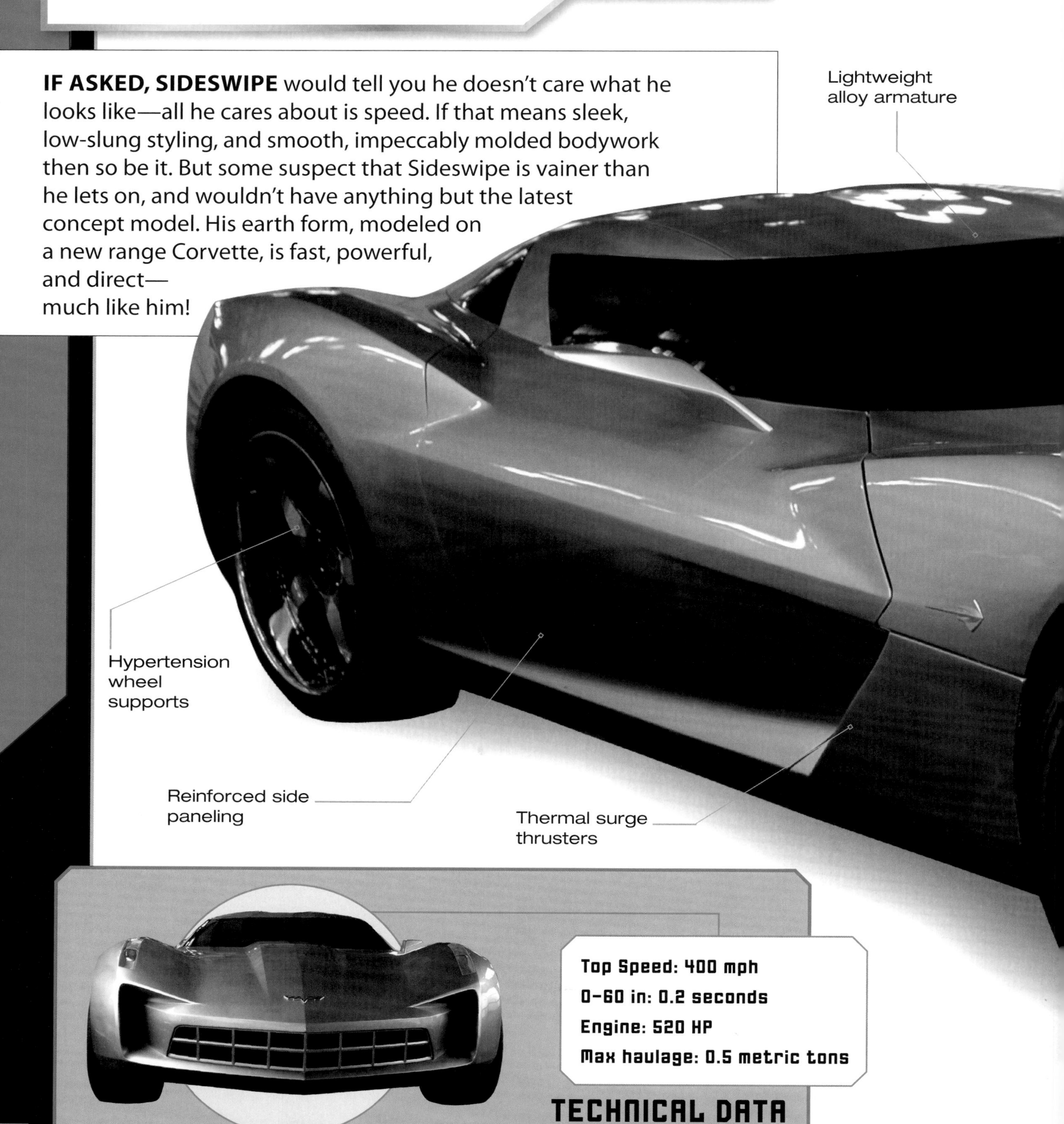

TECHNICAL DATA

Top Speed: 400 mph

0–60 in: 0.2 seconds

Engine: 520 HP

Max haulage: 0.5 metric tons

DID YOU KNOW?
Sideswipe is a master of the rapid-fire transformation, constantly switching from vehicle to robot mode and back again, often in a matter of seconds, during high-speed chases. This makes him highly versatile in a built-up area, able to adapt in an instant to any new set of circumstances.

BUMPER CAR
Sideswipe opts for lightweight metals and few if any extra layers of armor plating, instead relying on speed and maneuverability to avoid battle damage. His only concession to heavy armor is the chassis plating on either flank, as Sideswipe likes to broadside the unwary and send them spinning off the road.

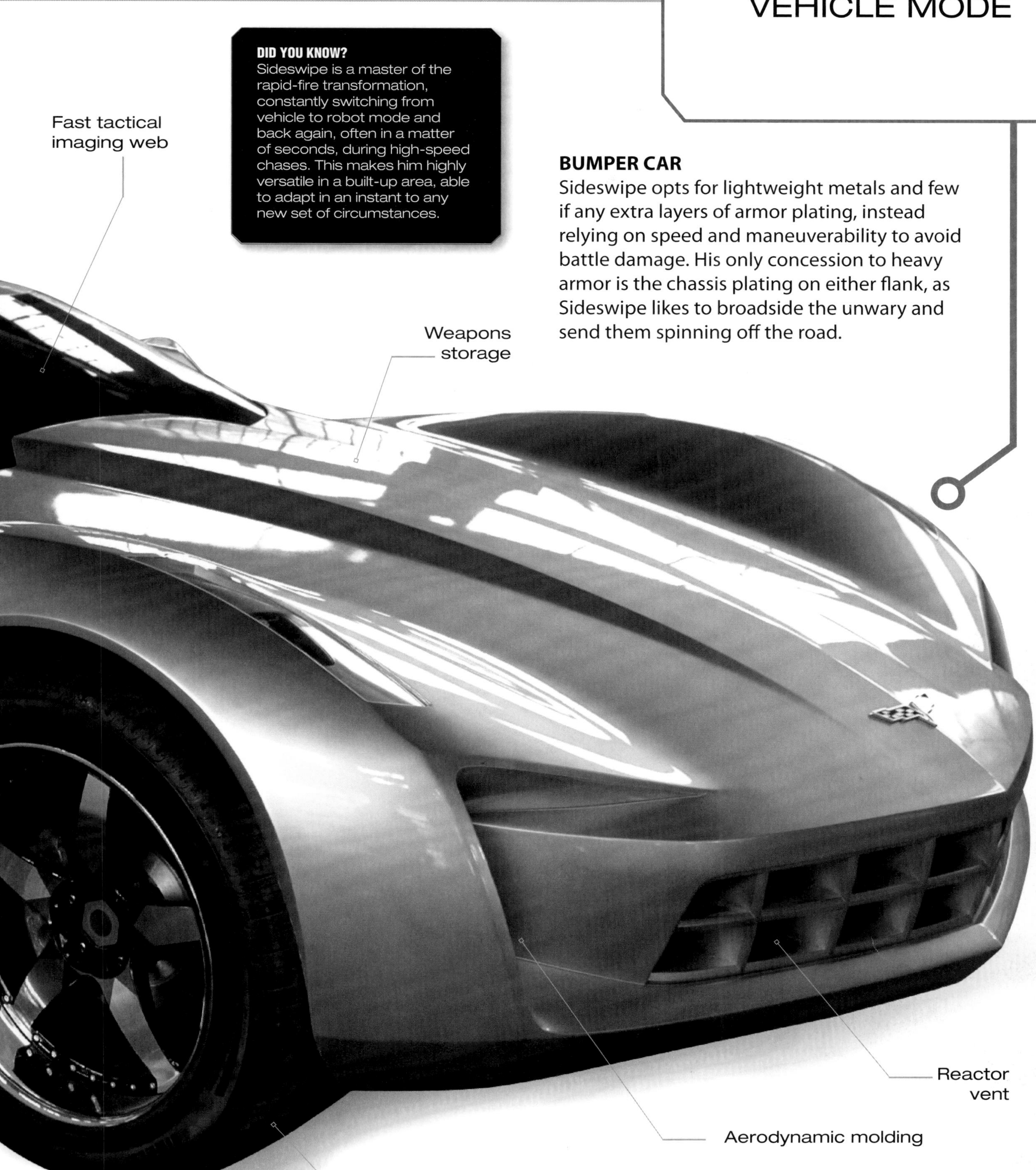

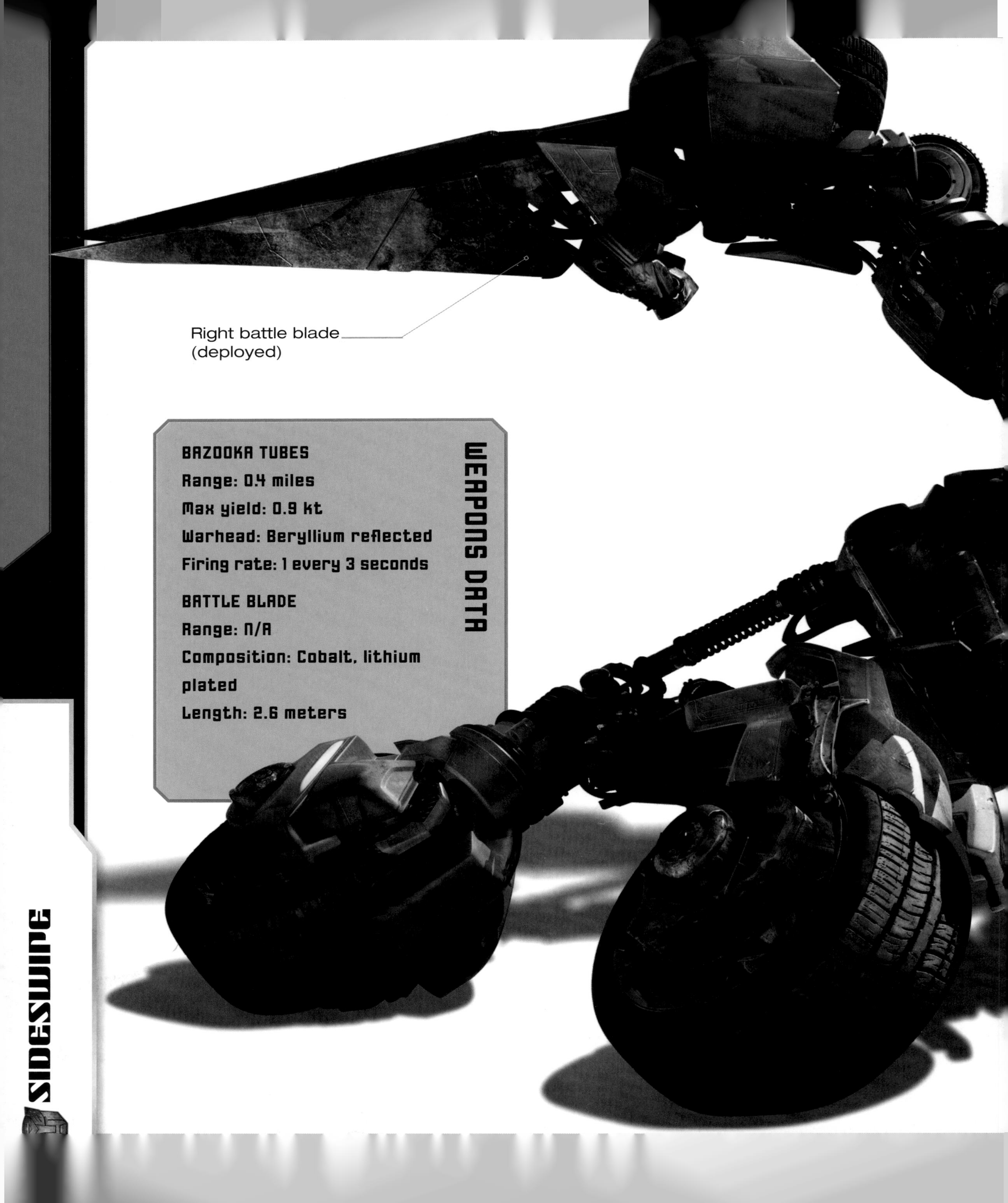

WEAPONS DATA

BAZOOKA TUBES

Range: 0.4 miles

Max yield: 0.9 kt

Warhead: Beryllium reflected

Firing rate: 1 every 3 seconds

BATTLE BLADE

Range: N/A

Composition: Cobalt, lithium plated

Length: 2.6 meters

SIDESWIPE
WEAPON MODE

THE SHEER LIGHTNING speed of Sideswipe is what makes him such an effective and deadly fighter. His slimline bazooka tubes and rapid-fire machine gun ports are weapons of last resort in Sideswipe's book. Most opponents are barely aware they're under attack before Sideswipe is on them, his battle-blades flashing with surgical precision. His wheel skates spin at 300 rpm, propelling him—for short, rocket-boosted bursts—up to a speed of 110 mph.

Left battle blade (deployed)

DID YOU KNOW?
Sideswipe has a highly sensitive internal balance gyro, allowing him to adopt attack posture angles of 70 degrees without simply skidding and crashing. This keeps him low to the ground and out of the line of fire, while further streamlining his aerodynamic attack run.

DEVASTATOR

WEAPON OF MASS DESTRUCTION

THE CONSTRUCTICONS ARE, individually, maestros of mayhem and purveyors of panic and pandemonium. But when large-scale demolition is called for, Hightower, Long Haul, Mixmaster, Rampage, Scavenger, and Scrapper team-up like never before—as Devastator! Together they are a rolling, crushing, catastrophic crew, flattening everything in their path. Interlocked in the form of a giant robot, this grunting, clanking engine of destruction will not rest until everything is rubble.

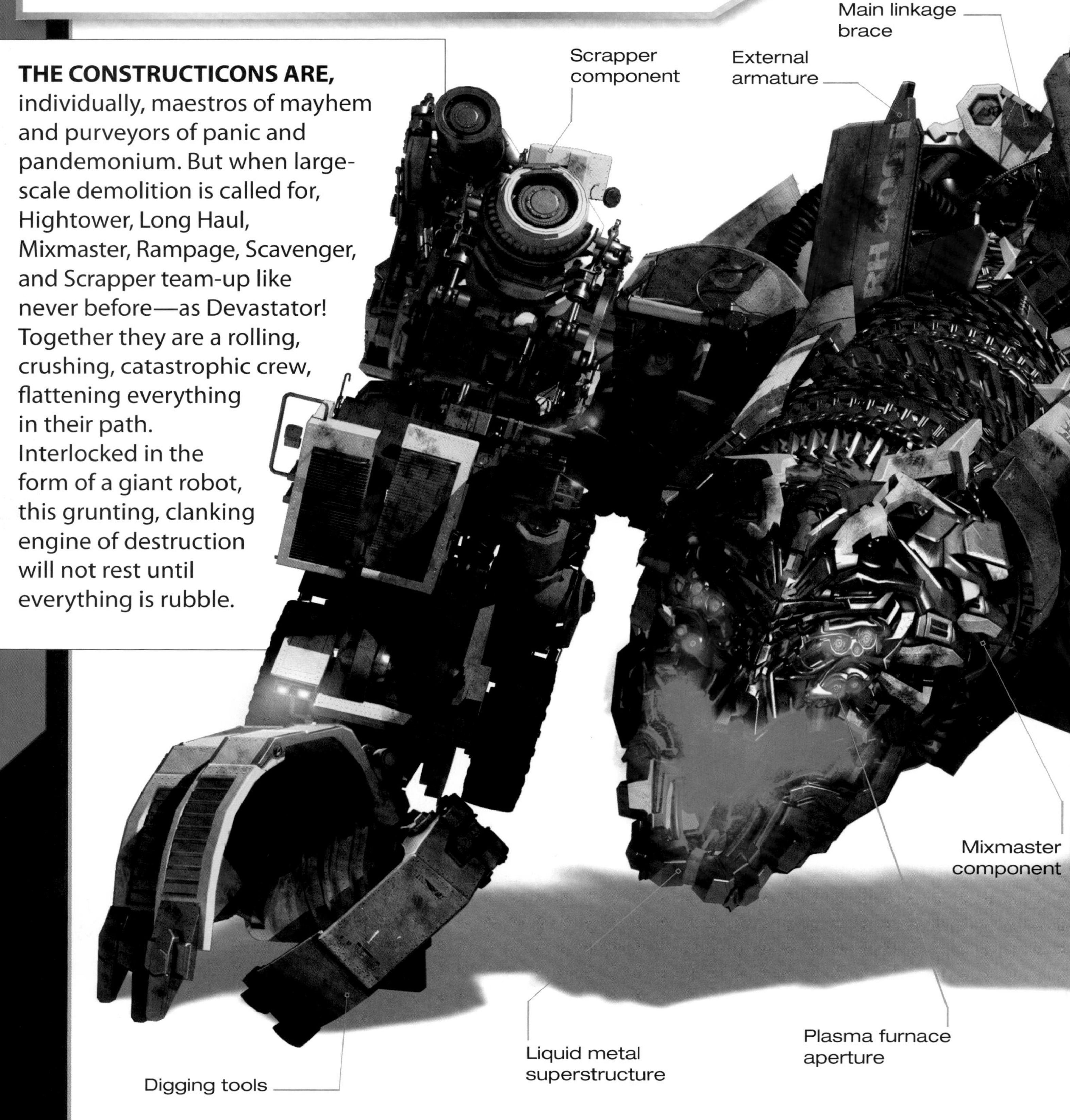

DEVASTATO
ROBOT MOD

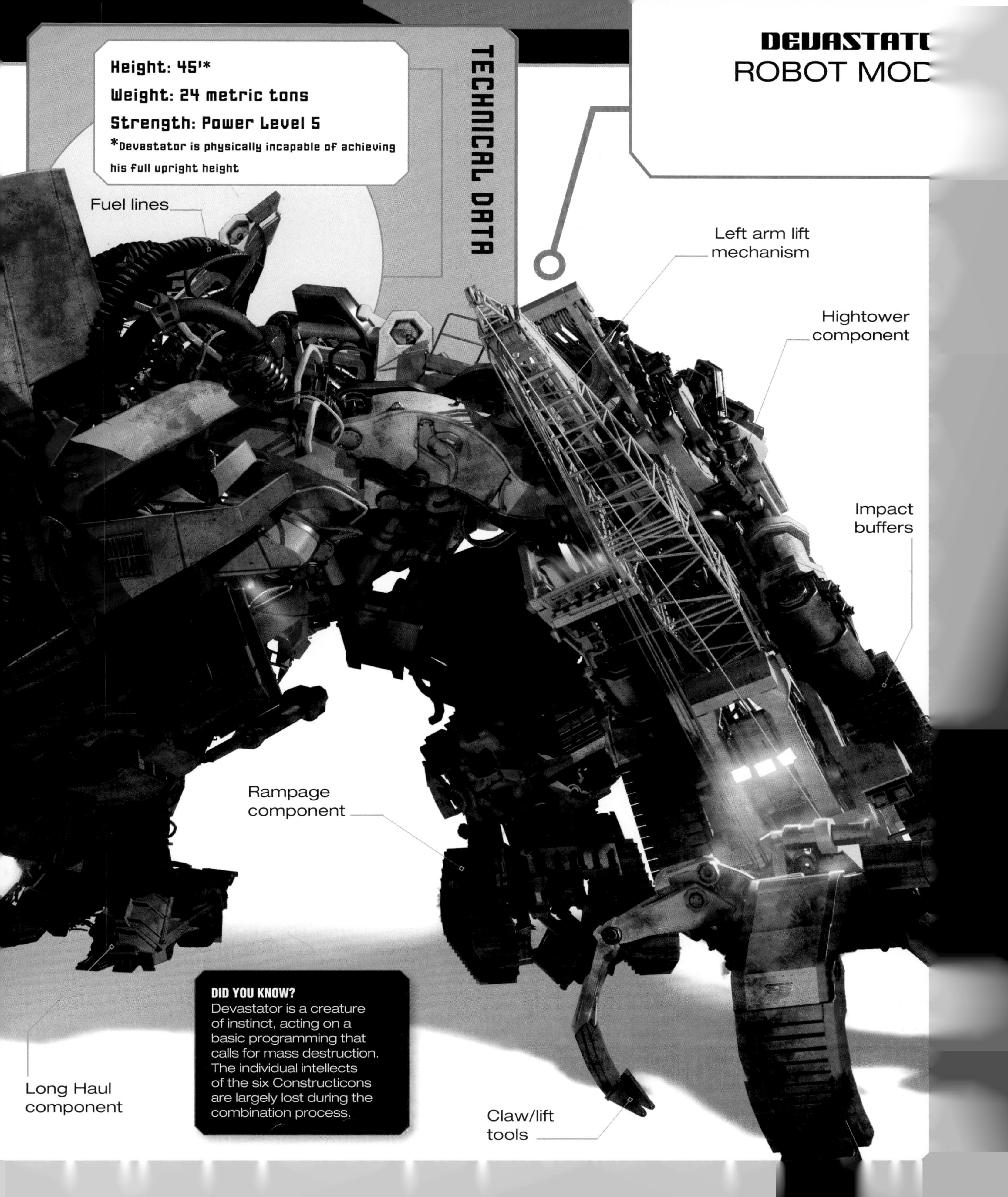

TECHNICAL DATA

Height: 45'*

Weight: 24 metric tons

Strength: Power Level 5

*Devastator is physically incapable of achieving his full upright height

DID YOU KNOW?
Devastator is a creature of instinct, acting on a basic programming that calls for mass destruction. The individual intellects of the six Constructicons are largely lost during the combination process.

DID YOU KNOW?
Devastator is an amazingly environmentally conscious weapon of mass destruction. Once his target has been reduced to rubble he automatically activates his internal suction vortex, ingesting huge quantities of metal and stone, which is then pulped in his grinders and reduced to a molten stew by the extreme temperatures in his plasma core. Useful minerals are extracted and the rest expelled as waste. The vortex ingestion process is also employed against living targets to great effect, and Devastator is at the forefront of any major offensive push by the Decepticons. Autobot siege entrenchments are targeted and breached and then Devastator activates his vortex funnel, sucking hapless Autobots up into his maw. Here they are broken down, and squeezed dry of precious energon, making Devastator entirely self-sustainable.

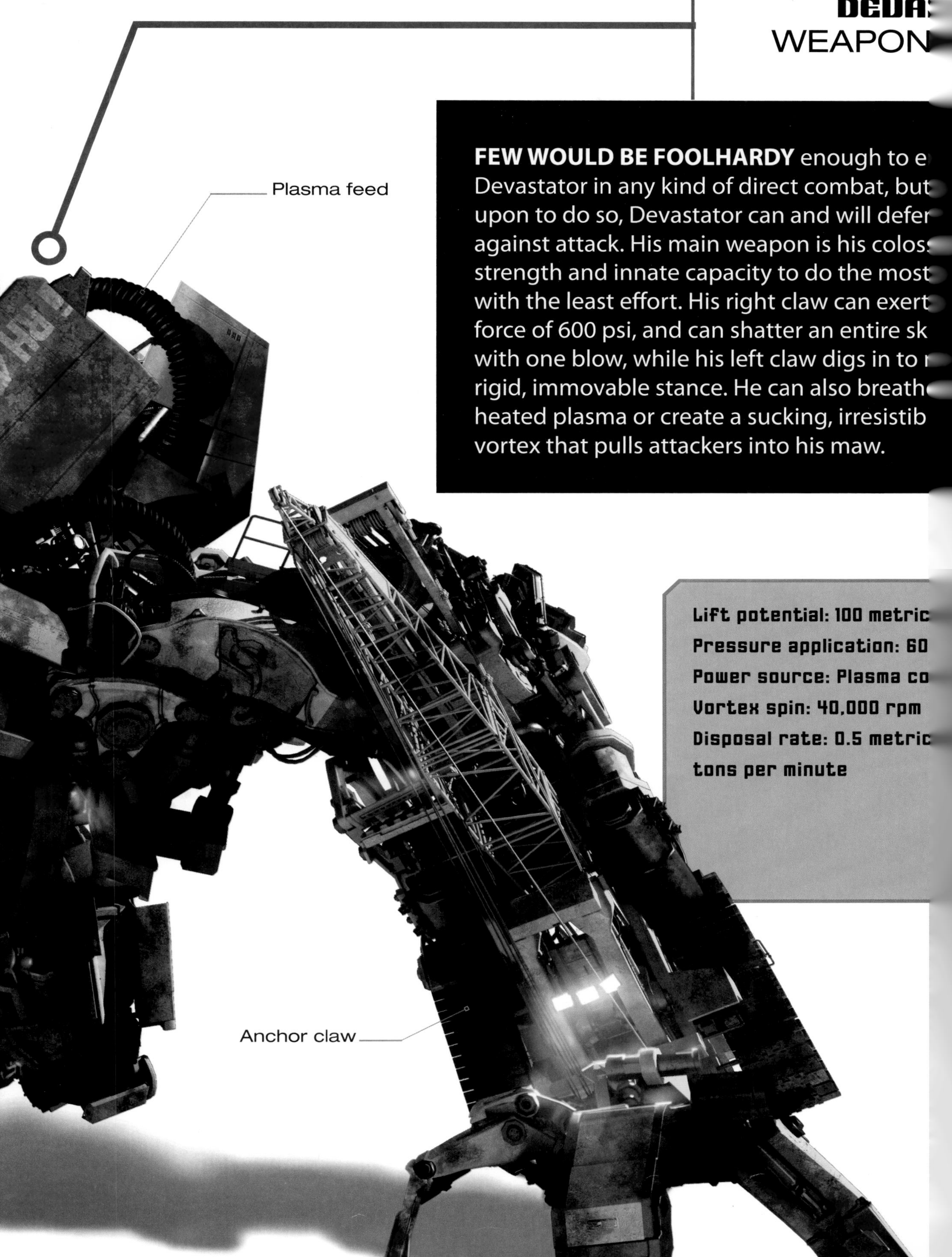

FEW WOULD BE FOOLHARDY enough to e
Devastator in any kind of direct combat, but
upon to do so, Devastator can and will defer
against attack. His main weapon is his coloss
strength and innate capacity to do the most
with the least effort. His right claw can exert
force of 600 psi, and can shatter an entire sk
with one blow, while his left claw digs in to r
rigid, immovable stance. He can also breath
heated plasma or create a sucking, irresistib
vortex that pulls attackers into his maw.

Lift potential: 100 metric
Pressure application: 60
Power source: Plasma co
Vortex spin: 40,000 rpm
Disposal rate: 0.5 metric
tons per minute

SKIDS/MUDFLAP

AUTOBOT INFILTRATORS

IN RARE CASES, a protoform splits in half and the Spark of life is divided between two Transformers. Skids and Mudflap are two such "twins," inseparable but usually at odds with one another. Hyperactive and noisy, they are chimerical by nature, and rarely settle into an alt. mode for long. They can even combine with each other, creating one more substantial alt. form.

"TOGETHER WE ARE MORE THAN THE SUM OF OUR PARTS."

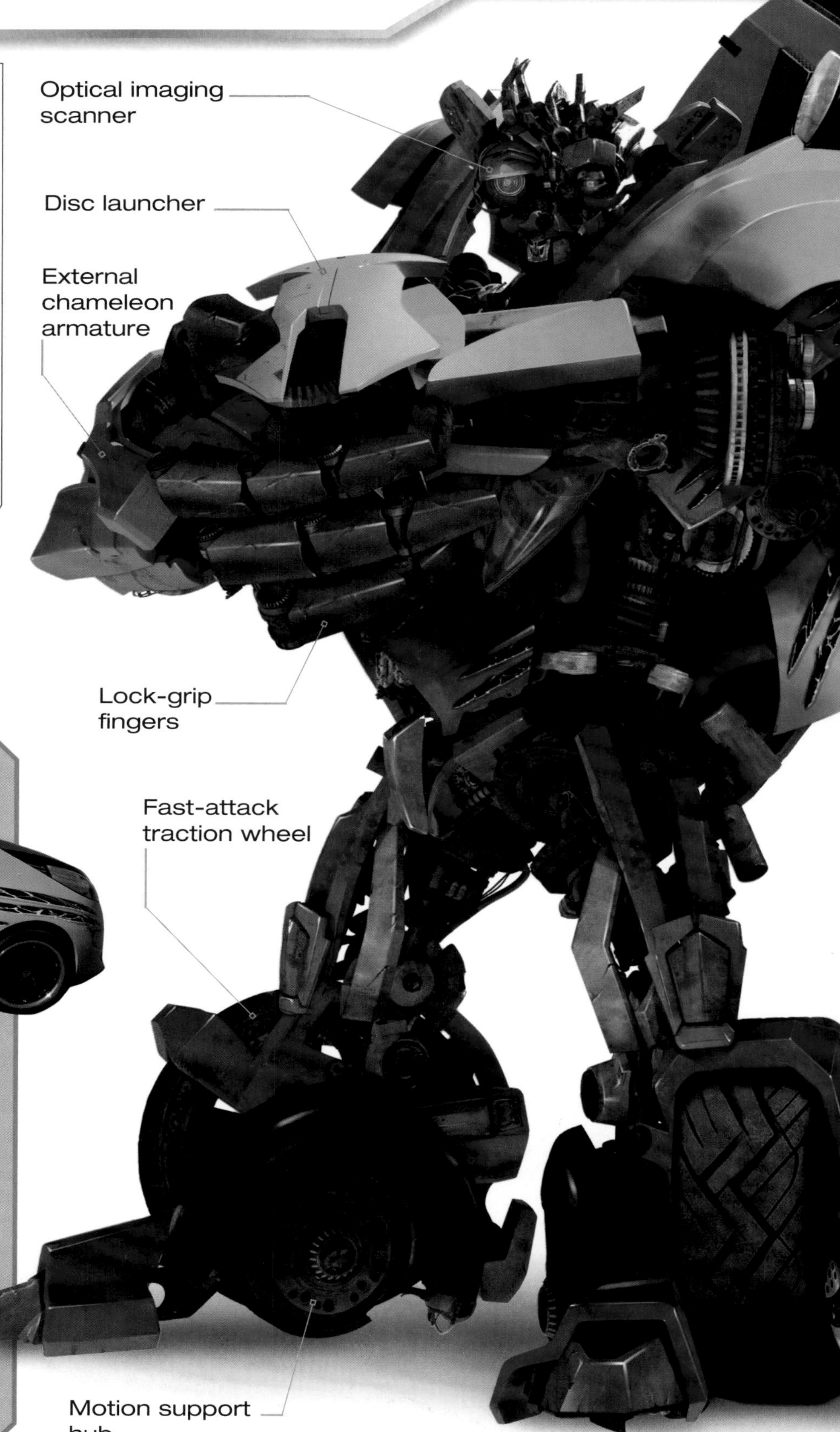

TECHNICAL DATA

Height: 11' 4"
Weight: 1.2 metric tons
Strength: Power Level 2
Top speed: 110 mph
0–60 in: 0.4 seconds
Engine: 180 HP
Max haulage: 20 metric tons

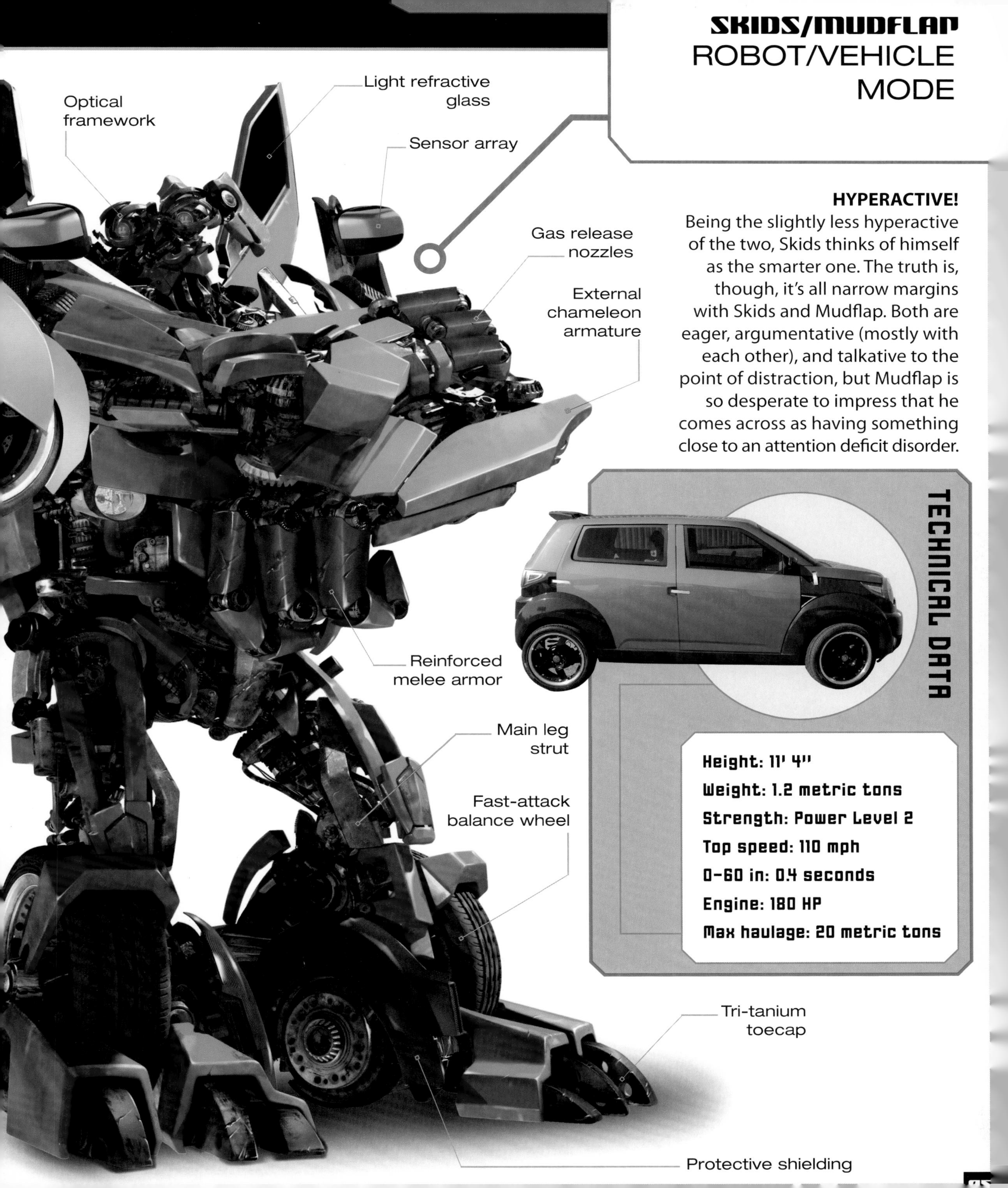

SKIDS/MUDFLAP ROBOT/VEHICLE MODE

HYPERACTIVE!
Being the slightly less hyperactive of the two, Skids thinks of himself as the smarter one. The truth is, though, it's all narrow margins with Skids and Mudflap. Both are eager, argumentative (mostly with each other), and talkative to the point of distraction, but Mudflap is so desperate to impress that he comes across as having something close to an attention deficit disorder.

TECHNICAL DATA

Height: 11' 4''
Weight: 1.2 metric tons
Strength: Power Level 2
Top speed: 110 mph
0–60 in: 0.4 seconds
Engine: 180 HP
Max haulage: 20 metric tons

THE FALLEN
OMNIVERSAL TYRANT

FROM A LOST ERA of exploration and colonization comes The Fallen, one of the most supremely powerful beings to stride the cosmos. Part of a glorious and noble lineage, The Fallen betrayed and butchered his brother Primes, disowning his given name in favor of one befitting his new, terrifying appearance. Within his cage-like exo-structure burned primal and chaotic forces drawn from the very birth of the universe, forces that expunged any last vestiges of conscience or morality, leaving only a pitiless void.

PRIME DIRECTIVE
It was the quest for Energon that drove The Fallen to take action against his brother Primes. While they were united by a directive that safeguarded all life, The Fallen did not care for the primitive organic creatures he encountered on Earth and so prepared to harvest its sun. In the battle that followed, The Fallen was imprisoned in a pocket dimension where he could do no immediate harm.

TECHNICAL DATA

Height: 42'
Weight: 9.1 metric tons
Strength: Power Level 5+

Energon distribution arc

Clutch grip exo-structure

Combat plates

DID YOU KNOW?
The Fallen can open and close spacebridges (dimensional portals) at will, drawing on his almost limitless power. These allow him to travel short or long distances in a microsecond.

ROBOT MODE

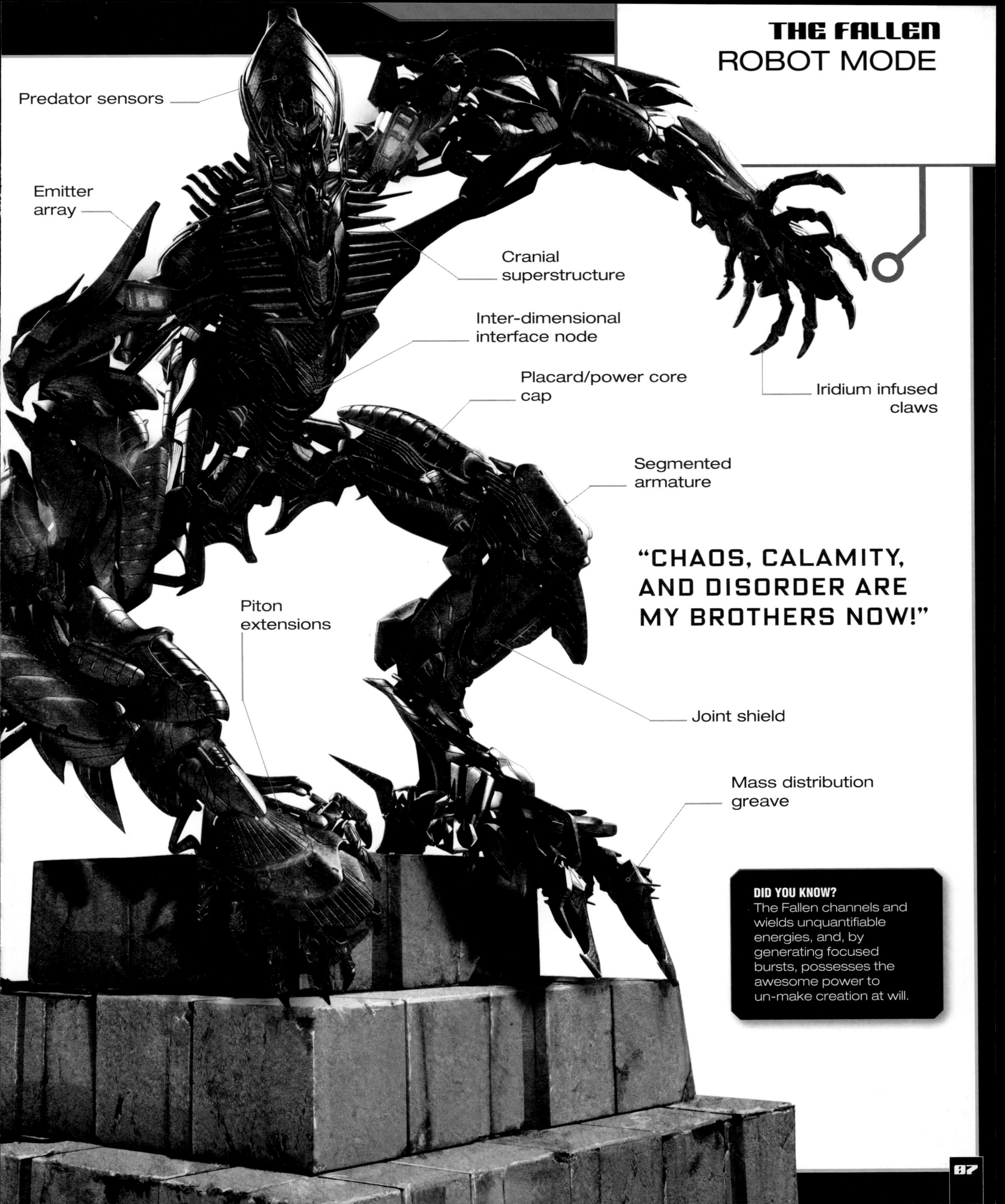

"CHAOS, CALAMITY, AND DISORDER ARE MY BROTHERS NOW!"

DID YOU KNOW?
The Fallen channels and wields unquantifiable energies, and, by generating focused bursts, possesses the awesome power to un-make creation at will.

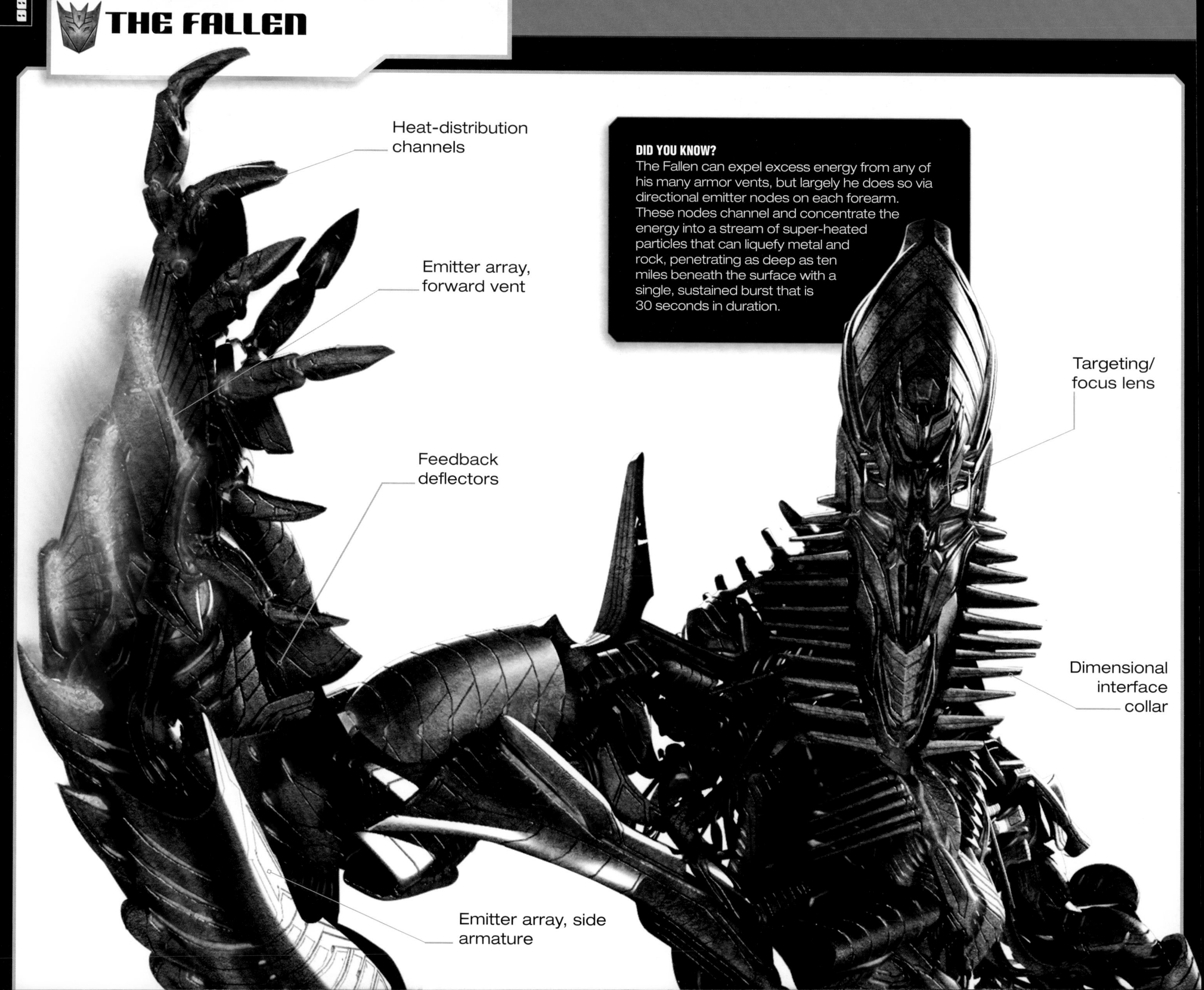

DID YOU KNOW?
The Fallen can expel excess energy from any of his many armor vents, but largely he does so via directional emitter nodes on each forearm. These nodes channel and concentrate the energy into a stream of super-heated particles that can liquefy metal and rock, penetrating as deep as ten miles beneath the surface with a single, sustained burst that is 30 seconds in duration.

WEAPONS DATA

EMITTER ARRAY
Range: No defined ceiling
Max yield: No defined ceiling
Energy source: Big Bang
Burn rate: 88 kilojoules per second

THOUGH WARPED AND TWISTED, The Fallen has the staggering power, strength, and resolve of a trueborn Prime at his disposal. Only now this awesome might is augmented by chaotic energies plundered when the universe was just forming. No physical form was ever meant to contain such forces, and to maintain his corporeal existence The Fallen must regularly vent

RAVAGE
DECEPTICON INFILTRATOR

NO ONE TRULY knows how much of Ravage operates as an individual and how much is simply a mobile extension of the living Decepticon data hive known as Soundwave. Certainly, when in the field on specialist infiltration or reconnaissance missions, he demonstrates such guile and acumen it's hard to believe an innate intelligence is not at work. Ravage responds to threats with an alacrity that is breathtaking to behold. He is a master of camouflage, stealth, and evasive maneuvers.

DID YOU KNOW?
While primarily a stealth agent, Ravage has a variety of offensive options on tap, from his spinning tail flail with 600-volt electrical spike to his built-in machine guns. Ravage also stores a swarm of nanotech-based secondary agents within him.

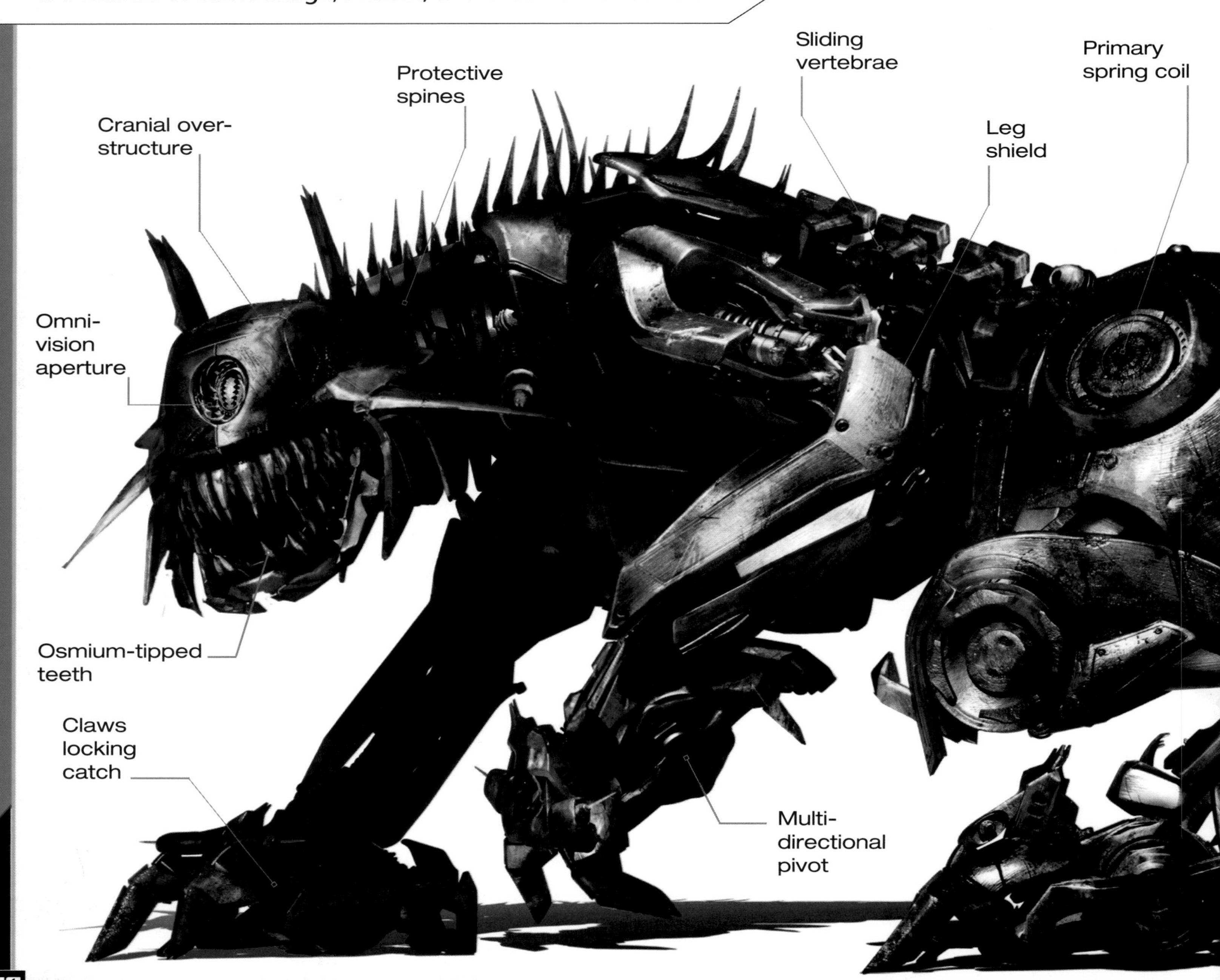

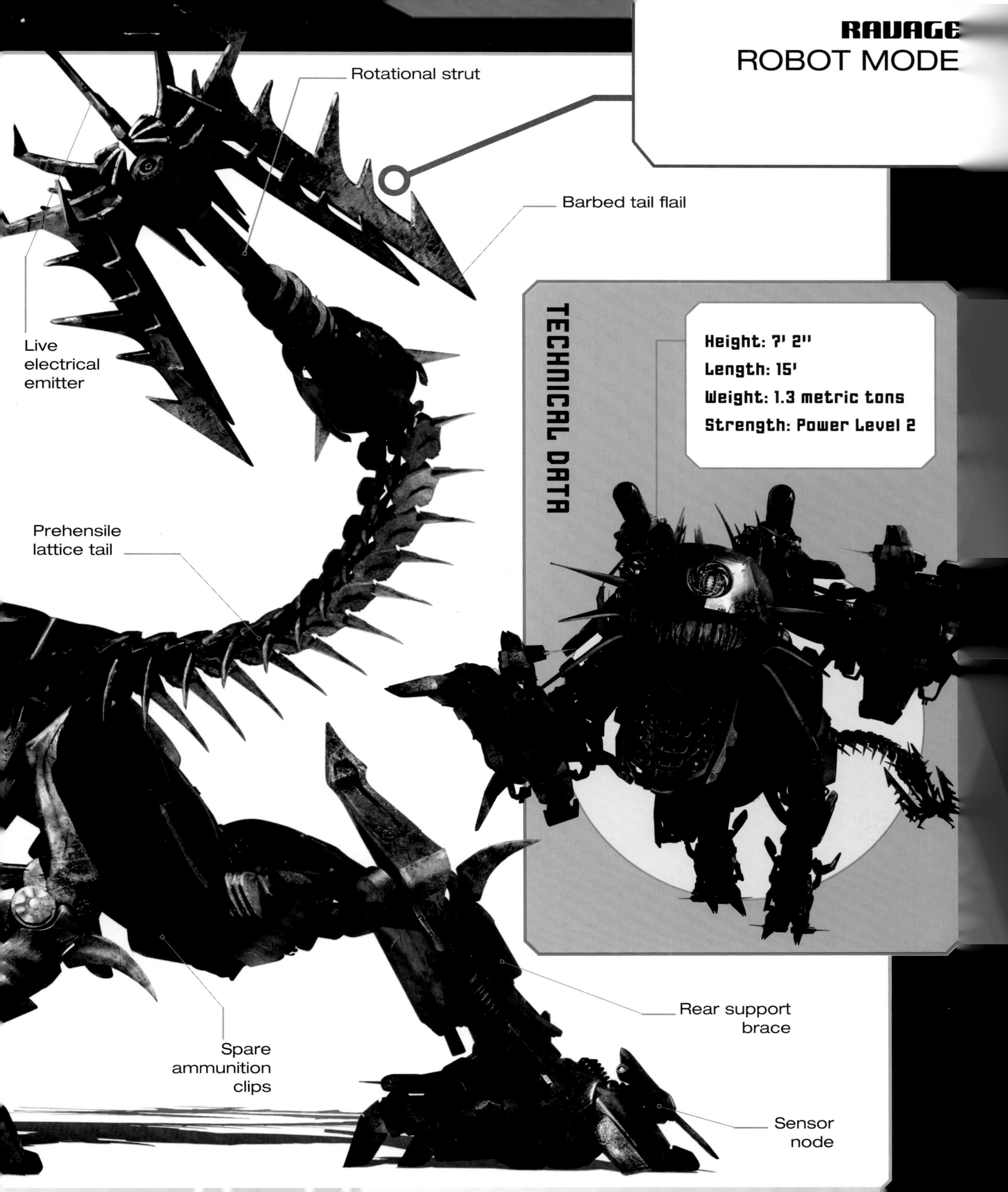
RAVAGE
ROBOT MODE
Rotational strut
Barbed tail flail
Live electrical emitter
Prehensile lattice tail
TECHNICAL DATA
Height: 7' 2"
Length: 15'
Weight: 1.3 metric tons
Strength: Power Level 2
Rear support brace
Spare ammunition clips
Sensor node

JETFIRE
SEEKER

CANTANKEROUS AND ORNERY, Jetfire is a warrior of the old school, believing in rules of engagement and fair play. It was this that led him to abandon the Decepticons and defect to the Autobots (although somehow he never quite got around to changing his insignia). Part of a group of so-called Seekers, despatched to Earth by the Fallen long before the arrival of the current Autobots and Decepticons, Jetfire—in what he stubbornly perceives as his "dotage"—has gone into semi-retirement, as a permanent "living" fixture of Washington's Smithsonian Institute.

"WITH AGE COMES WISDOM... AND RUST PATCHES."

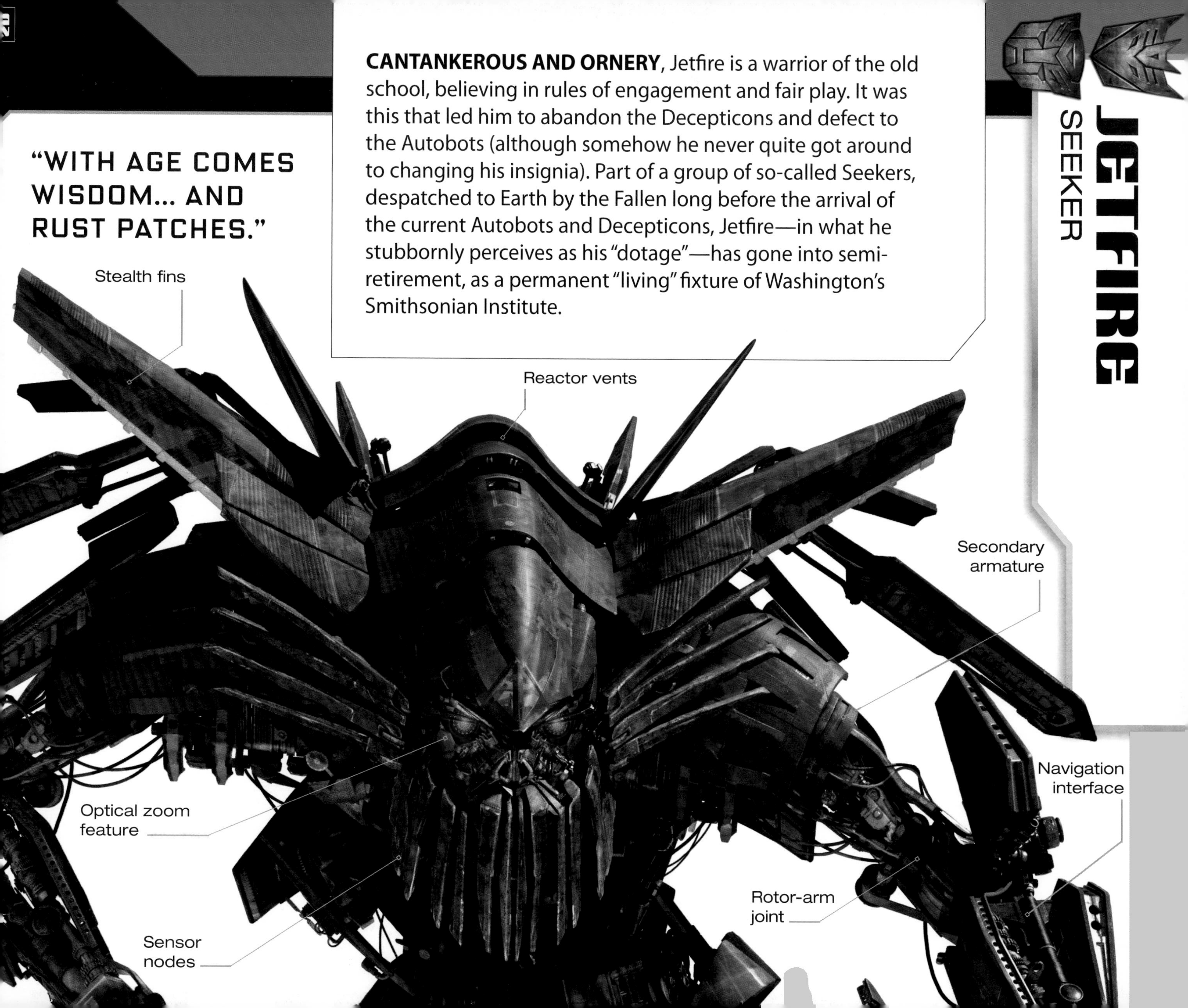

JETFIRE
ROBOT MODE

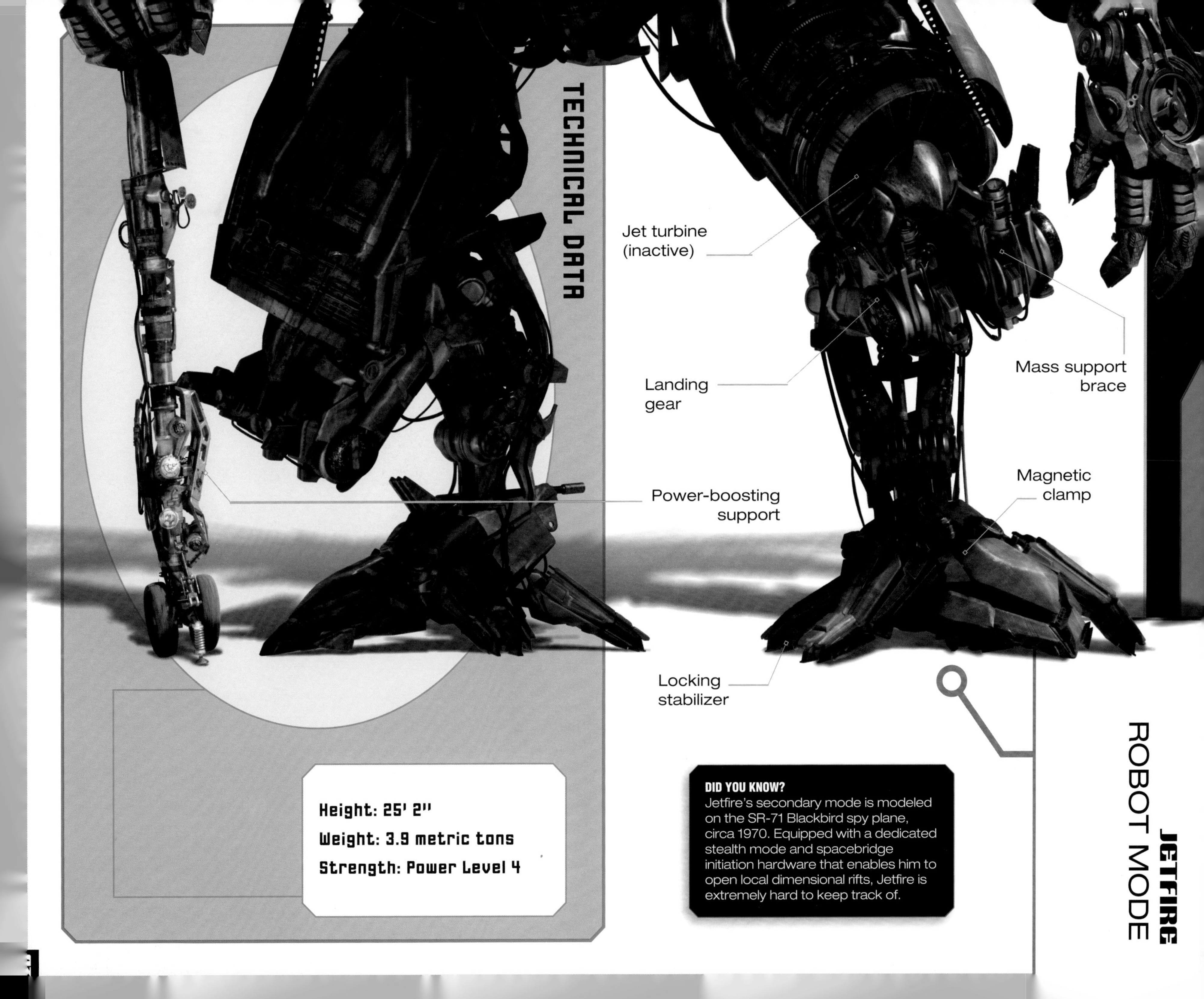

DID YOU KNOW?
Jetfire's secondary mode is modeled on the SR-71 Blackbird spy plane, circa 1970. Equipped with a dedicated stealth mode and spacebridge initiation hardware that enables him to open local dimensional rifts, Jetfire is extremely hard to keep track of.

TECHNICAL DATA

Height: 25' 2"

Weight: 3.9 metric tons

Strength: Power Level 4

ACKNOWLEDGMENTS

AUTHOR ACKNOWLEDGMENTS

OF COURSE, THIS BOOK could not have been written without access to the movie scripts for *TRANSFORMERS* (2007) and *TRANSFORMERS: REVENGE OF THE FALLEN*, and I am therefore indebted to the stellar work of authors Robert Orci and Alex Kurtzman. Thanks also to Aaron Archer and Michael Kelly at Hasbro, who provided so much essential background information on the new characters and IDW's Chris Ryall, who involved me so greatly in the prequel comics, which in turn provided so much of the formative groundwork for the characters and institutions featured in this book. And, as always, thanks to the legions of loyal TRANSFORMERS fans, without whom none of this would have happened at all.

DK WOULD LIKE TO THANK Ed Lane, Michael Kelly, and Amie Lozanski at Hasbro for their assistance.